A Myrtle Clover Christmas

A Myrtle Clover Cozy Mystery, Volume 21

Elizabeth Spann Craig

Published by Elizabeth Spann Craig, 2022.

This is a work of fiction. Similarities to real people, places, or events are entirely coincidental.

A MYRTLE CLOVER CHRISTMAS

First edition. October 25, 2022.

Copyright © 2022 Elizabeth Spann Craig.

Written by Elizabeth Spann Craig.

Chapter One

"**I** have to say you sound cranky, Miles," said his octogenarian friend, Myrtle. "I don't think you're quite getting into the tree trimming spirit."

Miles, who was indeed cranky, muttered, "That's because it was quite a hassle getting your plastic tree set up. There were myriad limbs and none of them seemed to want to go in their intended slot."

"It's something of a pain, I know. I probably should have tried to get Dusty to take care of it, except I already have another project in mind for him."

Miles raised his eyebrows. "Does the project have anything to do with gnomes?"

"It certainly does. Plus, I went to the dollar store and got the most adorable Santa hats. They're intended for children, so I believe they'll fit my gnomes' heads very well."

Miles's already-raised eyebrows soared even higher. "That must have cost you a fortune. You have a ton of gnomes."

Myrtle said, "But they were three to a pack. And I didn't get enough for *all* the gnomes. Just some of the more-visible ones out near the front of the pack. I do believe it would be fun to string lights among them, too, to highlight their dear little faces."

"Red will be sure to love it," said Miles dryly. "What sort of infraction did he commit this time?"

Myrtle's son Red was not only the police chief in the small town of Bradley, North Carolina, he was also the official thorn in her side. "He's been especially impertinent lately. Red seems to want me to surrender my driver's license, of all things."

Miles raised his eyebrows. "I'm assuming that has to do with the incident last week when you borrowed my car."

"It's not *my* fault that everyone is in such a hurry when they're driving. It's better to drive carefully and look out for pedestrians and children and whatnot. Besides, speed limits aren't a *suggestion*. It says *limit* for a reason."

Miles said, "Red told me that other drivers were having accidents while trying to pass you."

Myrtle shrugged. "As I told Red, if the state of North Carolina doesn't have a problem with me driving, then Red shouldn't either. Getting on my nerves appears to be his hobby. But it's Christmas, so I've been especially patient."

Miles hid a smile. Patience and Myrtle were not necessarily two words that normally went together.

Myrtle reached into a box and pulled out a feisty-looking snowman, putting him carefully on the tree. "Anyway, it's practically Christmas now and you're as late putting up your tree as I am. Turnabout is fair play; I'll help you put up your tree."

"That will be easy. I don't have one."

Myrtle looked appalled. "What? No tree?"

"I *did* have one. But I gave it away last summer when I was reorganizing."

Myrtle said, "I *thought* I'd seen a tree at your house these past years. Why on earth would you give it away?"

"It took up a good deal of space. and it was troublesome to put up, like this one." Miles gave Myrtle's tree a reproving look, as if it should try harder to cooperate next time. "I'm going with a minimalist look this year. I'm sticking with a wreath on the door."

"How positively Scrooge-like of you, Miles. A wreath is no fun at all. You can't even see it from the inside your house."

Miles was ready to change the subject. And fortunately, one of Myrtle's ornaments was begging for discussion. "Speaking of no fun at all, this ornament is particularly frightening-looking. What's the story behind this?"

Myrtle peered at it. It was a misshapen Santa head with wide, staring eyes and a crooked, rather sinister mouth. "Oh, that's something Red made when he was a little guy. I always put it up on the tree."

"You don't have nightmares, looking at it?"

"Certainly not. It's merely childish art," scoffed Myrtle. "It reminds me of the happy days when Red was both little and manageable."

Miles carefully put the ornament on the back of the tree, where he couldn't see it from the living room. "Are you ready for the wedding tonight?"

Myrtle said, "I suppose I am. It sounds rather dressy, doesn't it? The problem with dressy things is that one has to have something appropriate. My wardrobe is more geared to funerals than to weddings."

Myrtle's hairdresser, Faith, was getting married. It was quite the town event—a Christmastime wedding. Faith's aunt, who'd raised her, was giving it, and there'd been lots of chatter in the small town of Bradley about the event.

Miles said, "I'd think your black slacks and a dressy top would be fine. No one really cares what we wear, anyway. All eyes will be on the bride."

"That's true. Of course, you have it easy. A dark suit, which works for both weddings *and* funerals."

"Perhaps we'd better stop talking about funerals," said Miles nervously. "It might be tempting fate." He picked up another rather frightening ornament, studied it, and then carefully put it back in the box.

Myrtle was about to comment on Miles's pickiness when it came to decorating the tree when there was a knock on the door.

"I hope it's Dusty. I asked him to deal with the gnomes as soon as possible."

But when she opened the door, it wasn't Dusty's weather-beaten face she saw, but Wanda's.

"Wanda!" Myrtle said to her psychic friend and Miles' cousin. "What a wonderful surprise. Did you know Miles and I were decorating?"

Wanda gave her a tired grin. "Kinda thought you might be."

"Come on in," said Myrtle, motioning Wanda's thin frame inside. "Let's get you a snack. You can help us trim the tree. Miles is being extraordinarily picky about it all, and I'd like to finish decorating this afternoon."

Wanda brightened at the word *snack*.

Myrtle said, "Come on, Miles. You probably need a snack, too, after putting that tree together."

Miles looked a bit wary as he followed them into the kitchen. "Have you been baking?"

"Hmm?" asked Myrtle. "Oh, you mean the snacks? No, I've just been the lucky recipient of other people's efforts. Apparently, the town of Bradley is trying to cut back on sweets. Red has had folks bringing cookies, brownies, and whatnot by the station. He appreciates the gesture, but is worried about his waistline. He's brought most of them to me. It's the only redeeming thing he's done lately."

Miles, looking more cheerful, sat with Wanda at the kitchen table. Myrtle pulled out what looked like a vintage crocheted tablecloth in red, green, and white and placed it over the round table. She handed them Christmas plates and then loaded containers of goodies in front of them.

"The fudge is especially good," said Myrtle. "I'd probably stay away from the fruitcake. The cake is far too thick and the nuts are rather odd."

Wanda and Miles exchanged looks at the thought of Myrtle as a food critic. However, they obediently avoided the problematic fruitcake.

"Now Wanda, please tell us—are you here for a visit? To warn us about something the Sight has indicated? Or maybe you need some sort of help?"

Wanda swallowed down the entire Christmas cookie she'd put in her mouth. As she did, she seemed to be considering how to answer. "I sorta do need help. But it's not a real big deal."

"Of course it is! If you need help, we're here for you," said Myrtle stoutly.

Miles unconsciously put a hand to his wallet, as if he could feel it getting lighter.

Wanda took a deep breath. "It's jest that Dan is gonna spend Christmas with our cousin, Rumsey. 'Course, he's my cousin, too, but I jest don't like him."

"Then we don't like Rumsey either," said Myrtle immediately.

Wanda warmed to her subject. "Rumsey and Dan will drink too much, start singin', and git obnoxious."

"That doesn't sound like Christmas to me," said Miles. "That sounds rather like a party in a mead hall."

Wanda looked as if she wasn't entirely sure what Miles was talking about. But she gave a nod of her head, just the same.

Myrtle frowned. "Well, you simply can't be at home by yourself for Christmas. How awful that would be. You know you're welcome to stay here in that tiny guest room of mine. I just need to clear it out. It's been something of a staging area for me for that wedding we're going to tonight. I have clothes all over the place."

"I can clean it up," said Wanda quickly, wanting to make herself as useful as possible.

"Of course you won't! You're my guest. Cleaning up is outside of a guest's purview. Now, the only trouble is, is that Miles and I can't bring you along to that wedding tonight. Neither of us got a 'plus one' on our invitation."

Miles said rather regretfully, "People seem to think that we're beyond dating age."

Myrtle said, "In my case, they'd be correct. I'm still not entirely sure how you wangled an invitation to this wedding to begin with. The bride is my hairdresser, and we've been friendly, so that's how I'm on the list. But how are you on there?"

Miles said glumly, "The groom is in my chess club. He asked me in person if I could come, and I wasn't mentally agile enough to come up with an excuse not to."

"Don't wanna go to no wedding, anyway," said Wanda quickly. "Ain't brought nuthin' to wear." She paused for a minute, looking concerned. "Maybe you shouldn't go, neither."

Myrtle peered at her. "Is there a *reason* we shouldn't go?"

"Might be." Wanda looked uncomfortable.

Miles said, "The problem is that we've already RSVPed to the event, and it's mere hours away. They have a place for us at the table and have figured out how much food and beverage we might consume."

"Miles is right," said Myrtle with a sigh. "We should go to the wedding. It's a pity, because now I'm in the mood to play cards with Wanda. Playing cards would be far superior to eating wedding cake, which is so often either too sweet or too bland. But since going is now a foregone conclusion, I suppose we should focus on more important things. Such as: do you have an overnight bag, Wanda? I can't help but notice that you don't seem to have anything with you."

Wanda looked down at her plate. "Didn't want to make you feel you had to take me in."

"Then we'll need to swing by your house and pick up some things for you," said Myrtle.

Miles grimaced a bit. There was no "swinging by" Wanda's house. Instead, it was quite a voyage into the country on an old, unmaintained highway with treacherous potholes yawning from the road at every turn.

Wanda demurred, perhaps having seen Miles wince. "I could jest wash this every day." She pointed down to a well-worn sweater and some rather disreputable-looking jeans.

Now it was time for Myrtle to wince. "If you don't want to go back home, let's go shopping. It can be my Christmas present to you."

Wanda seemed a bit alarmed at this proclamation. "Don't want you to spend money."

"It's Christmas! But I'm on a strict budget, so don't worry. It'll be the consignment shop and the dollar store."

"I suppose you'll be needing a ride," said Miles, looking resigned.

"Naturally. It would be quite a walk over there. And there's a chill in the air."

Miles raised his eyebrows. "It's 60 degrees Fahrenheit."

"Well, compared to our usual 80 degrees, it's a bit nippy. But let's finish with the tree before we go. I'll play Christmas carols."

Wanda was looking at the Christmas tree with a wistful expression on her face. Myrtle turned on the music and said, "Wanda, will you help us out? Many hands make light work."

"Ain't done this in a while," Wanda said as she peered into the ornament box.

"Decorated a Christmas tree? You and Dan don't put one up?"

Wanda shook her head sadly. "For a while, there was too much junk in the house to put a tree up. Then I couldn't find the tree. Buyin' another one was too expensive. Then we got out of the habit."

"Well, you can share in this one."

The three of them put up Myrtle's old ornaments. Miles carefully hung the more objectionable homemade ornaments toward the back, Wanda put each one up with a great deal of thought, and Myrtle quickly slung ornaments on the boughs as fast as she could. In the background, Bing Crosby crooned about being home for Christmas.

"There!" Myrtle said finally. "The ornaments are all up." She frowned, glaring at the tree. "Something doesn't look right. Something is completely wrong."

Miles stood back, looking at the tree critically. "It looks all right to me."

But Wanda said in a hesitant voice, "Ain't there supposed to be lights on it?"

"For heaven's sake," said Myrtle. "Miles, we forgot the lights!"

Miles looked very much as if he had a terrible headache. "There weren't any strands of lights out anywhere."

"We must have left the box of lights in the hall closet," said Myrtle. "Now we'll have to take all the ornaments off to get the lights on it."

"Perhaps it doesn't need any lights," suggested Miles. "Perhaps it looks great just the way it is."

"Of *course* it needs lights. Wanda and I will want to see their cheerful glow when we're here at the house drinking hot chocolate and listening to Christmas music."

Sometime later, the tree was undecorated, strung with lights from the forgotten box in the closet, and redecorated.

"It does look much better this way," admitted Miles. "Despite all the bother. And now, if you're wanting to shop, we should go ahead and head out. That wedding is quickly approaching."

Chapter Two

Miles drove them to the consignment store, getting out of the car, but not following them.

"Aren't you coming in?" asked Myrtle. "I was planning on having Wanda do a fashion show."

Wanda looked as if she'd rather *not* do a fashion show. Miles gave her a sympathetic look. "I think I should go to the coffee shop a couple of doors down if I'm planning on being awake during the wedding. And perhaps the shopping will go quicker if Wanda decides which garment works best while she's still in the dressing room."

Myrtle looked doubtful at this but said slowly, "I suppose so. We lost a bit of time with the tree. I have my phone, so I'll just call you when we need to head to the dollar store."

Myrtle and Wanda walked into the store. Myrtle eyed the racks of clothes with a critical eye. "I'm thinking you need a variety of different things. A few tops, a couple of pairs of pants, something slightly dressy, something to hang around the house in, undergarments, and pajamas."

Wanda looked worried. "That sounds like a lot. Mebbe we should get Miles to drive me back home after all."

"Nonsense. Each piece of clothing is three dollars at the most. According to my mental calculations, we should be able to do this fairly cheaply."

A saleswoman wearing red glasses and a pair of reindeer antlers cleared her throat. "We've also got a Christmas sale going on. Everything is thirty percent off."

"Gracious! I can't even do the math on that, but that means everything is a good deal lower. Let's get cracking."

It wasn't long before Wanda had a complete, if limited, wardrobe in a cheery plastic consignment store bag. And some of the lines of worry had eased from Wanda's features.

Myrtle had called Miles right before they headed to the checkout counter, and he was in the parking lot by the time they exited the building. The next stop was the dollar store where Wanda picked up any toiletries she needed and Myrtle found a few stocking stuffers for her grandson, Jack. Myrtle pulled out her purse to buy Wanda's purchases, but Wanda shooed her hand away. "I got this one," she said with her gap-toothed grin.

Miles was dozing in the car when they joined him. He yawned and said, "Back to the house? I was just getting in a little nap since we're going to be up late tonight with the wedding."

"Let's head back to the house. We should watch our soap opera. I love it when the show is all Christmassy. Would you like to watch it, too, Wanda?"

Wanda considered this. "How about if I sorta watch it and sorta play solitaire?"

"That sounds like an excellent plan for someone who doesn't know all the convoluted backstories of the show," said Miles.

So that is what happened. Myrtle and Miles watched as Felicity and Adrian, brother-in-law and sister-in-law, hooked up rather implausibly at a family Christmas party. The family Christmas party, naturally, was at a mansion done up with a tremendous tree that took up most of the set. They were all wearing fabulous red clothing.

"I could see that coming," murmured Myrtle.

"Felicity and Adrian? How? It's very scandalous," said Miles.

"Because this is a very scandalous show. Plus, the set had mistletoe hanging all over it as foreshadowing. No one at that Christmas party could stand anywhere without being under mistletoe. It was a forest of it."

Wanda had apparently gotten quite sleepy during her solitaire game and had fallen asleep, her head resting on her folded arms. She was gently snoring.

"Poor thing. She deserves a bit of rest," said Myrtle.

After the show wrapped up, Wanda was still sleeping. Miles slipped out and Myrtle put a soft blanket around her before going into the back to put her feet up, herself. She'd *thought* she was going to just stretch out and work on her crossword puzzle, but before she knew it, she was fast asleep too.

Myrtle's eyes grew wide as she looked at the clock. It was time to get ready for the wedding and she still had very little concept of what she was planning to wear. She walked into the living room where Wanda was rubbing her eyes and looking as if she'd just woken up. Her eyes also widened when she looked at the clock.

"I guess our shopping expedition wore us out," said Myrtle, making a face. "Either that, or Miles drugged the decaf we had when we came back."

Wanda grinned at the idea of an errant Miles. "Can't picture that."

"No. So I suppose we were tired. Which is *fine*, but now I'm in a tizzy because I have to get ready for this wedding and I don't have the foggiest idea what to wear. Can you point me in the right direction?"

Wanda looked doubtful. "Ain't much with fashion stuff."

This was clearly true, but Myrtle was in desperate straits. "Just give me your opinion. Everyone will be looking at the bride, anyway."

So Wanda followed Myrtle down the short, narrow hallway to Myrtle's closet.

"I think the black slacks are a given. But what top should I go with?"

"How dressy is this weddin'?"

"Very dressy, I think. But my days of wearing ballgowns are over. Besides, I should just meld into the background."

Wanda picked out a white blouse that had sparkles on it.

Myrtle considered it thoughtfully. "The only problem with white is my propensity to spill things on whatever garment I'm wearing. That's why the black slacks were a given."

Wanda pointed to a red top with sparkles.

Myrtle tilted her head sideways. "It's kind of loud, isn't it?"

Wanda shrugged her thin shoulders. "It's Christmas, ain't it?"

"Right you are. The red blouse it will be! I'll bring a small plastic container in my purse and will bring some wedding goodies back for you. You won't want to wait for them, though—make yourself whatever you want for supper. I want to say there's a frozen pizza in the freezer."

"Don't worry about me," said Wanda. "I'll be jest fine." She paused, frowning. "But I ain't gettin' good vibes about this wedding."

"Aren't you? Well, you know how weddings are. I'd rather go to a good funeral any day than a wedding. They're shorter and, often, less emotional than weddings. Besides, weddings can be rather stressful. And Faith—that's my hairdresser who's the bride—was telling me when she was doing my hair that her aunt has been a real bear during the whole process."

"Her aunt?"

Myrtle nodded. "Faith lost her mother in a car accident when she was just a wee thing. Her father ran off and so her aunt, Glynis, raised her. She's rather formidable. Apparently, even though she's a very wealthy woman and *wanted* to make the wedding a showcase, she complained about every nickel and dime."

Wanda drawled, "Sounds like she jest likes complainin'."

"Precisely. Faith said that she kept telling Glynis that she and Holden could have a simple wedding with only a few guests in attendance. But Glynis wanted the big do. She wanted it both ways—big and expensive and something she could complain about. Maybe that's why you've got a bad feeling about the wedding."

"Mebbe." But Wanda looked uncertain. "You'll be careful?"

"Me? Certainly. I'll have Miles with me. I'll watch my step, too, and make sure there's no silly falling. It will be dark and we'll be in a tent, so I'll be extra careful. I'm sure it will all be fine."

An hour later, Miles tooted the horn outside and Myrtle hurried out, cane thumping as she went. She'd impulsively wrapped wide red ribbon on the cane to make it more decorative.

"You look very appropriate for the season," said Miles.

"I'm all ensconced in red, aren't I? I thought my cane could be taken as a giant candy cane, at a distance."

Miles quirked a brow. Seeing as how the cane was dark brown, that seemed unlikely. "The sparkly blouse is a nice touch."

"Isn't it? Wanda helped me pick out my wardrobe. I'm not sure I could have done it without her help."

"And you've even got a Christmas handbag," said Miles as he backed the car out of the driveway.

"Yes. The best thing about the purse is its capacity to hold things," said Myrtle in a self-satisfied manner.

"You don't have a Tupperware container, do you?" asked Miles in alarm. "That doesn't seem to fit wedding protocol."

"Oh, it will be fine. No one cares what I do. Besides, I'm hardly going to camp out at the buffet line and put food in a plastic container. I'll simply fill my plate with far more things than I could ever eat and then surreptitiously squirrel the extras away."

Miles frowned at this.

"It's much better than being wasteful, Miles. It would be horrid to throw food away."

"No chance of that," muttered Miles.

"Besides, the food is for Wanda. And Glynis, who's paying for the wedding, is rich and rather unpleasant. I'll have no guilty conscience, I assure you."

Miles seemed slightly mollified, most likely because Wanda would be the beneficiary of any food that left the wedding.

"And where are you driving? We seem to be heading in the wrong direction," said Myrtle.

Miles slowed down, frowning at the road ahead of him as if it were somehow betraying him. "Aren't we going to the Methodist church?"

"It's the Presbyterian one. Then to Glynis's house for the reception."

"Not to the church hall?" asked Miles. "It seems like we usually end up at the church hall for receptions."

"For *funeral* receptions. Not weddings."

"It seems it would work just as well. Now we'll be stumbling around in the dark under tents," muttered Miles.

"There will likely be some stumbling going on, for sure. That's why most weddings aren't held in the church hall . . . because the bride and groom want to serve alcohol."

"I see," said Miles.

The Presbyterian church was beautifully decorated for Christmas. There were large wreaths on the door, poinsettias on the sills under the stained-glass windows, and a glowing Christmas tree with Chrismon on it.

handed Myrtle some money, which she stuck in her large Christmas purse alongside the container of food.

There was suddenly a cheer from the guests and the bride and groom appeared, looking flushed and excited. The guests swarmed around them to greet them.

"This is where I always stay back," said Myrtle. "I can't deal with a mob scene around the couple."

"Is there never *not* a mob scene around the couple?"

"Rarely. But at least it gets better."

There was a bellowing sound, and Myrtle and Miles turned.

"What on earth is that?" asked Miles.

Myrtle blinked. "I do believe that might be Edgar Ross—the long-lost father of the bride."

Chapter Three

"Long-lost?"

Myrtle said, "The sort of long-lost that everyone is grateful for. Wishes devoutly for. I remember teaching Edgar Ross. He was an absolute nightmare in every way."

"The sort you had to send to the principal's office all the time?"

"The principal's office? Absolutely not. I dealt with him myself. And assigned quite a few especially tiresome classics for him to read and write essays on." Myrtle's eyes narrowed. "I can't imagine anyone would have invited him here."

"You don't think he's gatecrashing?"

Myrtle watched as Glynis rose from her chair, eyes steely, and strode off to her brother. "Oh, I somehow think he is."

The bride watched with concern as her aunt approached her father.

"You don't think there'll be a scene?" Miles looked a bit anxious about the idea of a scene at a wedding.

Glynis's voice rose to the point it could be heard over the sound of the band. She shoved her brother, and he put his hands up, shrugging and laughing. And, noticed Myrtle, staggering a bit, too. Alcohol was definitely in play.

"There's a scene," said Miles with a sigh.

"Think of it as an extended version of *Tomorrow's Promise*." Myrtle took a sip of her tiny glass of wine.

"Poor Faith and Holden."

And indeed, Glynis's ire seemed to suddenly spread over the entire family. Uncaring about the very expensive party she was throwing and the prospect of potentially ruining it, she bellowed, "This is really the final straw. Did you invite this man, Faith? Your useless, despicable father?"

Faith, looking as if she wanted the ground to open and swallow her up, shook her head miserably.

"Then how on earth did he find out? I certainly didn't tell him. All you've done is cause trouble for me, Faith. I think about how much easier my life would be if I'd never even *had* a brother. *Or* a niece. And the man you've picked as your life partner?" Glynis sneered. "He's just as useless as your father is."

Holden, who'd been protectively holding Faith's hand during this tirade, stood up, shoulders squared, and fist clenched.

Glynis snorted. "What are you going to do, Holden? You're not man enough to stand up to me. Carry on with your wedding party. I'm going off for a smoke."

The guests, who'd all been in stunned silence, looked at each other as if not knowing how to proceed. Should they all leave? Should they commiserate with the bride and groom for having such a harridan for a family member?

The band decided to help make everything clearer. They'd been paid to play and play they would. They immediately started in, quite loudly, with an energetic dance song. And the guests, obediently, rose to dance. Quite a few people headed off to get more drinks.

Miles said glumly, "I'm suddenly wanting to head back to your place and play cards with Wanda."

"Let's finish our food first. Aside from sugary treats, I don't have a lot to eat in the house right now. I don't want to waste this plate of goodies."

Miles looked down at his plate. "I seem to have lost my appetite."

"That chicken will help you regain it. It's good stuff. Now come on, Miles, dig in."

As they ate, they noticed the guests getting more revved up. It might have been the alcohol or it might have been in reaction to Glynis's emotional outburst. But everyone swarmed the dance floor and the bar.

Miles commented. "It looks like Faith's father wasn't scared away."

Myrtle snorted. "Fat chance of that happening. Not when there's free food and booze. He'll be here until they turn out the lights and pack away the tents." She frowned. "In fact, it looks as if he's about to pass out right at his table."

Edgar did indeed look rather inebriated. He was slumped in his chair. As they watched, he lay his head down on his arms as if the dance music was making him relaxed instead of energized.

"The guests are getting pretty wild," noted Miles uneasily.

"They certainly are. I have the feeling they're going to have terrible headaches in the morning." Myrtle's voice was smug, in the manner of someone who had only consumed a small portion of a tiny glass of wine.

"Let's find the bride and groom and hostess, thank them, and escape."

"You sound quite fervent, Miles! And that might be easier said than done. There's quite a scrum of people to wade through."

Somehow, the two managed to locate and isolate both the bride and the groom, thank them, and wish them well. Finding the errant Glynis wasn't as easy.

"Where could the woman have gone off to?" asked Myrtle with great irritation.

"Maybe she went back in the house," said Miles, gesturing to the looming mansion above them.

"Well, that would be a silly thing to do. She spent an obscene amount of money on this party. You'd think she'd at least brood somewhere where she could enjoy it."

Miles frowned. "You don't think she's still off on her cigarette break?"

"She could have smoked an entire pack of cigarettes in this amount of time."

Miles said, "We've looked everywhere else. I say we give up and write her a nice note telling her we enjoyed ourselves."

"You just want to make yourself scarce because of the scene she made. But I'm curious now. I intend to find out exactly what's happened to her."

Miles said uneasily, "You're making it sound as if she's met with foul play."

Myrtle quirked her eyebrows. "Anything is possible. I remember another incident where someone on a smoke break ended up meeting her Maker. You'll recall the Bunco episode. Even if it wasn't foul play, she might have gotten herself so riled up that she's experiencing some sort of cardiac event. We could be the ones to find her medical help."

Thus, persuaded by the thought of being helpful, Miles accompanied Myrtle to the area where Glynis was last seen heading off with her cigarette.

Myrtle gripped her cane, steadying herself as she carefully trod into the darkness. "There's not so much lighting here," she grumbled.

"They might not have expected anyone to be traipsing around in the woods."

Myrtle said, "That was rather shortsighted of Glynis, considering she's fond of a smoke." She paused. "That over there—what is it?"

Miles peered into the darkness, pushing his glasses up his nose as if they might help him. "What . . . the lump over there? Maybe a pile of brush."

"Very optimistic of you, Miles. Unfortunately, I have the feeling it might be a lump of something else. Or some*one* else. Can you turn on your cell phone flashlight?"

It took a bit of struggling with his phone for Miles to bring the app up. "I rarely use that one," he muttered. "I like real flashlights."

"Fair enough, but real flashlights aren't commonly brought to weddings."

Miles carefully shone his flashlight app ahead of them and they picked their way across the ground to the lump.

It was Glynis, dead.

Chapter Four

Miles stooped beside Glynis's body, ensuring that she was as dead as she seemed. He nodded and said in a gruff voice, "She's gone."

"For heaven's sake. And someone *did* this. It doesn't look natural to me, does it to you?"

Miles said, "I'm no medical professional, but the champagne bottle next to her and the wound on her head would seem to indicate that she was murdered."

"True. She certainly didn't go into the woods with a bottle. I'd have noticed that."

Miles said, "Do you have your phone handy? Call Red. Now that I've found my flashlight app, I don't want to turn it off to make the call."

Myrtle fished her phone out of her large handbag. When Red picked up, there was a lot of laughing and ruckus going on in the background. "Mama?" he asked.

"Are you at a party?" asked Myrtle.

"Are you?" he asked.

Myrtle supposed it *was* rather loud on her end, as well. The band was playing and there was cheering, hooping and hollering going on in the background for some reason. "I'm at Faith and Holden's wedding reception. But Red—Miles and I found Glynis, dead."

There was a groan on the other end of the line. "Oh no."

"It does appear to be murder."

Red said grimly, "I'll be right there. Don't touch anything and stay back."

Myrtle put her phone away and said, "I think we should at least stay in the vicinity. Someone should guard Glynis's body and ensure no one interferes with evidence."

"Someone should also probably direct Red where to go when he gets here."

Myrtle said, "An excellent idea, Miles! Perhaps you should stand near the driveway."

Miles frowned. "I don't want to leave you alone here."

"Alone? There must be two hundred people at this reception."

Miles said, "And one of them is a killer who might return to the scene of the crime."

Myrtle didn't have a chance to respond because a voice called out from behind them, "Glynis? Glynis, we're about to cut the cake."

Myrtle turned, and Miles winced. It was Faith, the bride and Glynis's niece.

Faith stood still. Her face was as ashen as the beautiful wedding dress she was wearing. She was a tall, pretty girl with jet black hair and brown eyes, which were now staring ahead of her at the lump that Miles's phone was illuminating.

"Oh no," she breathed.

Miles gave Faith a wary look as she swayed on her feet. He hurried over and took her by the arm. "I don't think this is the best place for you to be right now."

"What happened?" asked Faith in a strangled voice. "Is she . . . dead?"

Miles looked pleadingly at Myrtle, and she quickly took over. "Faith, I'm afraid your aunt has met with foul play."

Faith's voice rose to a high pitch. "Foul play? What happened?"

"We don't really know yet, but I've called Red, and he's on his way over."

Sure enough, the faint sounds of a siren or two could be heard in the distance.

"We should move you back up to the party so you can sit down," said Myrtle firmly.

Faith said, "No. No, I think I should stay with her. It's the least I can do." She took in a rattling breath. "Someone told me that she'd taken a smoke break. I had no idea . . . this is so . . ."

Miles said, "I'll grab a chair."

Myrtle grasped Faith's arm while Miles did grab a chair, in the off-chance Faith's swaying became more pronounced.

"Where's Holden?" asked Myrtle.

Faith shook her head. "I'm not sure." Her lips pressed together, forming a thin line.

Myrtle frowned. "Weren't you both together at the reception?"

"No, there was a bit of a commotion up there." Faith gave a shaky laugh. "One of the groomsmen had too much to drink and the rest of the wedding party was trying to get him out of there. Then one of my bridesmaids started wailing about something because *she'd* had too much to drink and we were trying to calm her down."

"Perhaps that's all the commotion I heard," said Myrtle thoughtfully.

The siren grew piercingly closer as Miles put a chair behind Faith and she sank gratefully into it.

Faith said in a quiet voice, "I can't believe she's gone."

"There, there," said Myrtle. "It will all be fine."

Red texted Myrtle to narrow down her location, and she sent Miles up to direct him down into the woods.

Red bounded toward them, with Miles following along behind. He wasn't wearing his uniform, a fact which only confirmed to his mother that he had indeed been out at a party.

He gave Faith, still sitting in the white folding chair, a look of concern and then his gaze followed the beam from Miles's phone flashlight over to Glynis's body on the ground.

Miles cleared his throat. "Myrtle and I were looking for Glynis to thank her before we left the reception."

Red turned on his own flashlight and stepped closer to the body, his eyes narrowed as he took in the champagne bottle nearby. He turned to Faith. "I'm guessing the reception is being videotaped?" His voice was hopeful.

Faith breathed in. "You think she was murdered?"

"We'll have to investigate, but it does seem that way."

Another tear slid down Faith's cheek. "Glynis balked at paying for video, but we have a photographer."

"I'll want to speak to your photographer." Red glanced around. "Where's Holden?"

A rather defensive tone crept into Faith's voice. "He's visiting with the guests. I had my eyes on him the whole time before I came over here, though."

Myrtle lifted an eyebrow at this patent lie. Red looked at his mother thoughtfully, and Myrtle carefully made her expression blank again.

"I'm very sorry for your loss," said Red. "You and your aunt got on well together?"

Faith said in the manner of one who's repeating something she's said many times, "I'm very grateful to Glynis for raising me and taking me in. My father was always disappearing and wasn't there for me. If it hadn't been for Glynis, I'd have been in foster care somewhere."

Red said, "When I was walking in, I noticed Edgar Ross was here. He was invited?"

Faith snorted. "Absolutely not. I'm not even sure how my father found out about the wedding. The only reason he's here is because of the free booze. It has nothing to do with his feelings for me. If he'd had any, he'd have been around when I needed him, growing up."

Red nodded. "It must have been upsetting to have him show up."

"You have no idea," muttered Faith. Her gaze strayed over to her aunt again.

Red noticed the direction of her eyes and said, "Why don't we move you somewhere else, Faith. I can speak with you later."

Faith shook her head stubbornly. "Not until you get more of a team over here. I feel like I need to keep an eye on her."

Red nodded again. "I've got the state police on the way and my deputy is coming, too." He paused. "From the way I see it, weddings can be stressful things. There are a bunch of details and people have different ideas for the way they want things done. You and Glynis navigated all of that well?"

Faith sighed. "Well, there were a few tense moments, of course. Holden and I don't have a lot of extra cash, being as young as we are. At first, I was really relieved when Glynis offered to pay for the wedding. But then, she sort of took over everything and made it the way *she* wanted it."

Red tilted his head to one side. "Glynis has never had a wedding of her own, as far as I'm aware."

"That's right. I guess this was a sort of proxy wedding. Anyway, I just let her plan it as she wanted. But by the end, I felt bad about her pouring so much money into it." More tears streamed down her face. "And now look what's happened. It's all ruined."

Red gave his mother a questioning look, and Myrtle dug into her Christmas purse to pull out a packet of tissues. Faith took them, gratefully.

Red said, "Faith, do you have any idea who might have wanted to harm your aunt? Did she have any troubles with anyone recently? Any problems she told you about?"

Faith said bitterly, "Maybe it's my dad that's done it. He's always needed money. Maybe that's really why he showed up at my wedding—to get rid of his sister, so money will go to him."

"Would Glynis have provided for her brother in her will?"

Faith shook her head. "I don't think so. I think Glynis would have left it all to charity before she left a penny to my dad. But I haven't seen her will."

"Do you know if she has one?" asked Red.

"I don't, not for sure. But Glynis was so organized that it's hard to believe she wouldn't have made one. She's the kind of person who would have kept it updated, too."

They turned at the sound of Red's deputy calling out to him.

Red said, "Grisham, could you make an announcement that all the guests need to stay put? I need to speak with everyone before they leave."

Grisham looked concerned at this. "What kind of announcement?"

Myrtle rolled her eyes. Grisham never seemed like the sharpest tool in the shed.

Red said in a patient tone, "Just say that there's been an incident and ask everyone to stay put until we talk to them. If they ask questions, tell them more information will be disclosed at a later time."

The deputy bobbed his head and headed off. Red was about to ask Faith more questions when her new husband called her name in an anxious voice behind her.

"There you are," Holden said. "I've been worried about you. What's happened? Is everything okay?"

At the concern in her husband's voice, Faith burst into tears.

Red and Myrtle both gave Faith an alarmed look. Red hastily said, "Holden, Glynis is dead. Can you settle Faith over in the reception area somewhere? And I'll need to speak with you soon."

"Of course," said Holden gruffly, looking uneasily around until his gaze settled on Glynis. He stooped and put his arm around Faith, who was still seated in the folding chair. "Let's go sit at a quiet table under the tent, okay? I'll send someone to get you some water and something to eat. You haven't had a bite the whole time we've been here."

Faith nodded and stood up, leaning her head on Holden as he led her away.

Red looked relieved at her departure. Then he turned to his mother and Miles. "I definitely know where to find the two of you if I need to ask questions. You can both take off for home now."

Miles, who'd been ready to leave even before finding Glynis, accepted this with alacrity. "Ready, Myrtle?" he asked in a hopeful tone.

Myrtle nodded. "I suppose so. I'll have to write up what happened tonight for the newspaper, of course. It should be front-page news tomorrow."

Red raised his eyebrows. "Are you sure? It's rather late to make tomorrow's edition. Besides, I think Sloan is out at a Christmas party. I sort of doubt he's in the right shape to be able to re-do the front page at this hour."

"Did it happen to be the same Christmas party you were also attending?" asked Myrtle. "I was just wondering who might have invited you to a party and not me."

Red sighed. "It was Sloan's shindig, Mama. But you shouldn't get your nose out of joint over the lack of invitation. He knew you and practically everyone in town was going to be at this wedding. Besides, you absolutely terrify him. You wouldn't bring a relaxing ambiance to his get-together."

"Don't be silly. He's a grown man. I was his teacher decades ago. Maybe I make him *uncomfortable*, but I certainly don't terrify him."

Miles and Red exchanged a glance.

"All right, Mama. Anyway, he just had a few people over—some folks who write for the newspaper and a couple of other people. Like I was saying, he's imbibed too much, so he doesn't need to be staggering off to the newspaper office. You don't need to be writing crime stories for him, anyway. He was just telling me at the party how much people were looking forward to your helpful hints column. Do you have a Christmas edition?"

Myrtle looked sour at the very mention of the helpful hints column. "Sloan is obsessed with that feature, and I don't think it gets nearly the readership he tells people it does. I have the feeling it's the same crotchety old woman who tells him she loves it. But yes, I do have a Christmas-themed helpful hints column. It's full of fascinating details like ensuring you use stale popcorn for garlands because it's easier to thread."

"Don't look so glum, Mama. That's exactly the kind of tip that's going to make someone's Christmas easier." At the sound of cars pulling up, Red said, "That must be the state police. Time for you and Miles to head on out."

Miles happily strode away from the reception, but Myrtle grumbled under her breath as they went.

Miles was relieved that he was able to get his car back and that it appeared to be undamaged, despite the large number of vehicles around it.

"Well, that was a wedding to remember," he said wryly.

"I know. Poor Faith."

"Poor Glynis," said Miles.

Myrtle sighed. "I'm trying to summon some sympathy for Glynis, but I'm finding it increasingly difficult. She certainly didn't deserve to meet her Maker during a very expensive reception that she was throwing, of course. But she was definitely misbehaving during the party."

"She was making scenes, for sure."

"Indeed," said Myrtle. "But that's the sort of person Glynis was. She wouldn't address something to you in private. No, she had to call you out on it right then, regardless of the situation. She was a real straight-shooter."

"What are you and Wanda going to do now? Should I come and hang out for a while and play cards?"

Myrtle said, "I thought you were exhausted. You were practically falling asleep at the reception, despite all the loud music."

"I suppose our grim discovery and the thought there was a killer in our midst must have woken me up some. At any rate, I don't see myself falling asleep anytime soon. I should probably do something quiet to wind down a little."

Myrtle snorted. "I'm not sure playing cards will fit the bill. Perhaps you should try a game of chess with Wanda instead. Grab the board from your house and bring it over."

"What will you do, though?"

"Me? I'll write the story for the newspaper and present it to Sloan tomorrow. However, considering the deliberate way you and Wanda play chess, that will take only a fraction of the time. I'll work on the tail-end of my Christmas cards after writing the article."

Miles raised an eyebrow as he pulled the car into Myrtle's driveway. "From what I remember, you've got quite a long list of Christmas card recipients."

"I do. That's because once people get on my Christmas card list, they never come off it. You really have to present me with a death certificate before I'll remove your name. But I've been working on filling out cards for a while and I've just got a few last-minute stragglers left. Your chess game will provide me with plenty of time to make some good headway."

The evening progressed nicely, with Wanda and Miles happily playing chess, Myrtle knocking out the article and her Christmas cards, and Christmas carols playing in the background.

Chapter Five

That night, Myrtle slept restlessly, her dreams fraught with deadly champagne bottles, irascible aunts, and drunken wedding party guests.

Myrtle finally gave up on sleep and set about making breakfast at the improbable hour of four a.m.

Wanda staggered out into the kitchen, her hair sticking up on her head from having slept on it. "Kin I help?"

"Absolutely not. You're my guest, Wanda. Besides, breakfast is my specialty."

Wanda nodded. Breakfast was indeed Myrtle's specialty. In fact, it was the only meal she could prepare without ruining the food. Ordinarily.

Wanda drawled, "Didn't sleep last night?"

"Not much. And when I did, I had all sorts of really horrid dreams. Sometimes it's best to throw in the towel and just get up for the day." She frowned. "Besides, I have some business with Sloan to handle."

"That story?" Wanda yawned.

"Yes. I have the completed article for Sloan. I need to let him know it's being emailed over so that he can look for it.

I should also send over your latest horoscope with that same email. That will ensure he opens it."

Wanda raised an eyebrow. "Ain't got no horoscopes yet."

"Haven't you? After breakfast, I'll jot them down as you dictate them. Then I'll call Sloan."

Wanda glanced over at the wall clock, which had a crowing rooster on it. "Ain't it sorta early to call him?"

"What?" Myrtle peered at the clock. "It's 4:30 now. Surely a newsman gets up early in the day."

Wanda didn't look convinced.

A few minutes later, they dug into their breakfasts. Myrtle had made scrambled eggs, bacon, and cheese grits. "Pretty good, isn't it?"

Wanda grunted in approval.

After they finished and cleaned up, Myrtle found a notebook and pen and Wanda gazed thoughtfully into space.

She said, "Tell Ben Pritchett not to put the roof decorations up this year."

"That sounds ominous," said Myrtle, jotting it down in the notebook.

Wanda nodded. "He'll come flyin' right off that roof if he does. Tell 'im to jest put 'em on the bushes." She continued, "Sarah Covington better git her furnace serviced afore it stops workin.'"

"Excellent advice," murmured Myrtle. "Do you have any for me?"

Wanda looked somberly at her, a bit of sadness in her eyes. "You don't listen to it."

"What? I always listen very carefully to you. You're my friend."

Wanda muttered, "You listen and don't do anything."

"Not always true," said Myrtle. "Although perhaps somewhat true. I have the feeling you're about to tell me I'm in danger. I always pay attention when you tell me that. But you're right—I don't stop investigating. Is that what you were going to say?"

"Yer in danger." She hesitated. "An' if you want somethin' done, you gotta do it yerself."

Myrtle stared at her. "An interesting tip, for sure."

They finished with the horoscopes, and Myrtle looked at the clock again. "Well, we passed a little time, anyway. I think surely Sloan is up by now. I'm calling."

Sloan, however, didn't seem inclined to pick up.

"How annoying," murmured Myrtle as she hung up and tried again.

Once again, Sloan didn't pick up.

Myrtle frowned. "I'm thinking something has happened to Sloan. He doesn't take care of himself, you know. Perhaps something horrible has happened. Perhaps he's suffered a heart attack."

Wanda looked doubtful. "Might jest wanna sleep. Might have his phone turned off."

"Or he might be struggling to breathe and in dire need of medical assistance," said Myrtle, her imagination running away with her. "Maybe we should go over there and check on him in person."

"Ain't got a car," observed Wanda. "Too far to walk."

Myrtle pursed her lips. "I'll try to call him once more."

The third time was apparently the charm. Right before Myrtle was about to give up, Sloan suddenly answered the phone, sounding panicky. "Miss Myrtle? Has something happened? What's going on? What time is it?"

Myrtle said, "It's nearly six o'clock, Sloan. You've clearly overslept. I'm sure you're relieved that I woke you up."

Sloan, however, didn't sound relieved. In fact, he sounded exhausted. "Oh. Well, I was up late last night, you see." He yawned, a loud noise which made Myrtle pull the phone away from her ear.

"Yes, I heard about your party. I was very sad that I didn't merit an invitation. Considering I used to teach you and that I'm now a colleague of yours."

Sloan sounded fairly miserable on the other end. "Miss Myrtle, I didn't think you'd want to come. Besides, I figured you'd be over at that big wedding. Didn't you tell me the bride was your hairdresser?"

"Yes, that's where I was. But it still would have been nice to have been asked. At any rate, I didn't call to berate you on your horrific lack of manners. I covered the big story in an article. I'm sure you'll want it to run tomorrow on the front page."

"Big story?" Sloan paused. "Is that why Red left last night?"

"It is indeed. The bride's aunt was murdered last night at the wedding reception. I've written it all up. And, of course, I intend to provide continuing coverage of the story as things progress."

Sloan made a sort of groaning sound on the other end.

"Are you quite all right, Sloan?" asked Myrtle.

Sloan said, "I just have a little headache, Miss Myrtle. And I'm sorry to hear about the bride. But mostly, I'm sorry to hear that you're planning on covering a murder investigation. Red isn't going to be happy with me again. Besides, I had another story I was hoping you'd be taking care of for me. A holiday piece."

"What kind of holiday piece?" asked Myrtle, sounding suspicious. "It sounds fluffy. I don't do fluffy stories."

"It's not fluffy at all. It's a special feature."

Myrtle rather liked the sound of "special feature" better. "Okay. What's the topic?"

"Well, you know how it is in a small-town paper. If you mention a bunch of people in the town, you get a lot more papers sold. They buy extras for their scrapbooks and for their mama and just to have them at home. I figured if you went around and collected people's Christmas traditions, it might make for a great holiday article. Plus, it would sell a lot of papers."

Myrtle considered this. Ordinarily, this wasn't really the kind of story that she would want to work on. She didn't have a whole lot of interest in what other people were doing for Christmas. On the other hand, it would give her an excuse to speak with some of the suspects in the case. Once she figured out who the suspects were, of course. Having an excuse might prove handy.

"I suppose I *could* work on that story."

"Really?" Sloan's voice was delighted on the other end. "Gosh, that's great, Miss Myrtle."

"I'll work on it *in addition* to the continuing coverage I'm doing on the murder investigation," said Myrtle placidly.

There was a brief, disappointed silence on the other end. "That sounds like a lot of work, Miss Myrtle."

"Does it? It won't take me long, Sloan. Besides, it's not as if I have a very busy schedule. It'll be fine. I should go now. Hope you have a good day." And she abruptly hung up.

Wanda said, "Whatcha gonna do today?"

"That's precisely what I need to figure out—my plan of action. And we need to collect Miles. Surely he's up by now. It's practically daybreak."

Wanda glanced up at the rooster clock again and looked doubtful.

"I'll call him in a minute. I'm thinking that we'll deliver some food to Edgar Ross today."

Wanda croaked, "That's the dad of the bride you was telling me about?"

"Precisely. He just lost his sister, after all. And, while I'm there, I can ask him about his Christmas traditions for the paper." Myrtle paused. "Actually, I should ask you *your* Christmas traditions."

Wanda sighed. "Used to have 'em when Mama was still alive. Don't no more."

"What did you used to do? I won't put it in the paper unless you want me to. But I'm just curious."

Wanda's eyes had a faraway look in them. "Mama used to have a special meal for Dan and me. She'd save up a little while for it. All our favorite foods. Did it on Christmas Eve, not the day. Then we'd go to the service at the church. They'd have candles out." She looked wistful.

"And the traditions stopped when she passed away?" asked Myrtle with a frown.

Wanda shrugged a thin shoulder, but looked sad. "Tried to keep 'em up. But Dan didn't really want to do 'em anymore with Mama gone."

"I see." Myrtle sighed. "It can be tough to decide what to do with traditions after someone dies. Maybe this isn't such a fluffy article after all."

There was a tap on the door.

"Miles," said Wanda in the tone of someone who knows.

Myrtle hurried to the door and swung it open wide. Sure enough, Miles stood there, looking as if he might have been awake for quite some time. He was fully dressed with khaki pants and a button-down shirt.

Myrtle beamed at him. "I *thought* you might be awake! Come on in and have some coffee and hang out with Wanda and me. We were just talking about making a plan for the day. Sloan has given me a holiday puff piece to write and I plan on using it to interview suspects."

Miles looked wary. "Won't it be odd if you start by asking Christmas-related questions and then morph into murder?"

"Morph into murder. That sounds like a title for a TV series, Miles. How creative you are this morning! And no . . . I don't think it will seem odd at all. I'm an octogenarian. I'm allowed to rapidly change the subject."

Myrtle fixed Miles a cup of coffee while he considered what to say next. He finally said, "Maybe it would be interesting if you took Wanda around with you today. Folks love her, as you know.

And it will be a lot more interesting than her spending time here at the house, alone."

Wanda, however, was casting a longing look at the deck of cards.

"Is that what you'd like to do, Wanda?" asked Myrtle with a frown. "Because I'm thinking you have a somewhat stressful life with your nutty brother. Would you like to make the rounds with me as I conduct a murder investigation? Or would you rather hang out at the house, playing solitaire and watching junky shows on TV?"

Wanda gave her endearing gap-toothed grin. "Probably rather watch junky shows."

"See, Miles? You can't escape it. Besides, it will be fine."

"What excuse will *I* have for being there? You'll be there because of the article. Won't I sort of stick out?"

Myrtle said, "I'll introduce you as a cub reporter."

Miles looked very unhappy at this prospect.

"All right, then. A co-reporter. But your name won't be in the byline. I'm thinking we'll speak to Edgar Ross first. By all accounts, he wasn't invited to his daughter's wedding. Glynis was clearly displeased about his presence there. And he may think he stands to inherit a good deal of money from the death of his sister. We'll bring food to him, as well."

Miles looked alarmed at the thought of Edgar getting homemade food from Myrtle. But then he decided, from what he'd heard, the man likely deserved it. "What will you make?"

Myrtle pondered this. "Let's see. I have a very motley assortment of things in my pantry and fridge. I'm not too fond of going to the store this time of year. I definitely have tuna. And some canned French style green beans."

"Sounds delicious," said Miles with a straight face.

Encouraged, Myrtle continued. "Do you think tuna and green beans would go with canned diced tomatoes?"

"Why not?"

Myrtle said thoughtfully, "And then you need a crunch, don't you?"

"A what?"

"You know—most casseroles have something crunchy in them," said Myrtle.

"Do they?" Miles vigorously avoided indulging in casseroles whenever possible.

"Yes. I could sprinkle Ritz crackers on the top."

"*Whole* Ritz crackers?" asked Miles.

"Yes. That would deliver the crunch." Myrtle strode over to her pantry and pulled out canned items. "I'm going to throw it together. I love the creative process in cooking."

"Mmm," said Miles noncommittally.

As Wanda and Miles played cards, Myrtle mixed the tuna, green beans, and tomatoes together.

"It's a sort of funny color," said Myrtle, frowning at the concoction.

Miles drew from the deck. "Is it? Well, you'll put the crackers on top, won't you? That should hide it."

"An excellent point, Miles!" Myrtle carefully lay the crackers on top of the mixture and then popped it into the oven. "What temperature do you think? Since I'm not working from a recipe."

Wanda and Miles exchanged a look.

"Edgar is a bad guy, isn't he?" murmured Miles to Wanda.

She nodded. "Not very nice with family."

Miles called back to Myrtle, "I'm thinking 400 degrees for 45 minutes."

"Won't it be rather dry?" asked Myrtle.

"I think that's precisely the texture you're looking for. Besides, isn't there a lot of moisture in the dish? Did you drain the tuna and the vegetables?"

"Drain them? No. I wanted the dish to be succulent," said Myrtle.

Miles backtracked. "In that case, why not just leave it as-is?"

"You mean *don't* cook it?" Myrtle frowned.

"The ingredients are already cooked, aren't they? Everything is either canned or a cracker."

Myrtle nodded slowly. "I do believe you're right. You don't think Edgar will mind a rather soupy casserole, do you?"

"He'll be grateful for it. And it's so festive, too. It has both red and green colors in it for Christmas."

Wanda grinned at Miles and he gave her a wink as Myrtle beamed at her soupy casserole.

"Indeed it does. Good point, Miles," said Myrtle. "I'll just put some plastic wrap over it and we can go see Edgar."

"Do you know where he's living? It didn't sound as if his family would have invited him to stay with them."

"Oh, I'm sure he's at Glynis's house. He would have leapt at that opportunity as soon as he realized she was gone. We'll try there first."

Miles gave the clock an anxious look. "Are we sure he's awake?"

"Of *course* he is. The police are probably over there talking to him even as we speak. It'll be fine."

But as they knocked Glynis's front door some fifteen minutes later, no one answered.

Myrtle frowned. "Perhaps he's a little deaf. He did listen to a lot of loud music when he was young."

Miles's gave a soft sigh as Myrtle pounded on the door and rang the doorbell many times in a row.

The door suddenly flew open and a wild-looking man with hair standing on end gaped at them. He looked, Myrtle reflected, rather like Crazy Dan, Wanda's brother.

"Edgar," said Myrtle. "Miles and I wanted to extend our sympathies for your sister's death. We brought a casserole."

Edgar rubbed his eyes and peered closely at Myrtle. "Well, I'll be. If it ain't Miss Myrtle. I thought you was dead."

Myrtle flinched at the *was*. "And I thought I taught you English. It appears it didn't take."

Edgar yawned. "Sorry. I just woke up. I'll try to talk better." He paused. "Uh, do you want to come in?"

Chapter Six

Myrtle was already sweeping through the door with Miles trailing behind her. Glynis's house was quite large by Bradley standards. She had the feeling it was ordinarily quite neat, as well. Now, however, Edgar had clearly already left his mark. There were empty beer cans on the coffee table, shoes scattered around the living room, and sofa pillows on the floor.

"Housekeeper's day off," muttered Edgar with a rusty-sounding laugh.

Myrtle and Miles perched on the sofa, and Edgar pulled a chair up.

There was a quiet pause in the conversation before Edgar said, "Uh, nice of you to come by. Too bad about Glynis."

He didn't seem very upset by his sister's sudden demise. Myrtle said, "Were you up very late last night? When did the police let everyone leave?"

Edgar considered this. "Oh, it was probably a couple of hours or more. Were you there?"

"Miles and I were in attendance, yes. However, because we'd discovered your poor sister, we spoke to the police first and were able to leave soon after."

Edgar's eyes opened wide. "What? What were you doing out in the woods?"

"Miles and I were attempting to thank Glynis for hosting us at the reception."

Edgar snorted. "On her smoke break? Y'all were pretty brave. As I remember it, Glynis wasn't one who liked being interrupted when she was trying to smoke. Especially if she was already mad. And she was, because she'd had that big blowout."

"With your daughter and her new husband," said Myrtle.

Edgar chuckled. "Yeah. But you know, Glynis would take on anybody. And she never did care if it was in public or not. I remember she launched an attack at me when we were eating out at a restaurant years ago. I never saw it coming."

"Did the two of you get along well?" asked Myrtle. "I didn't teach your sister."

Edgar had a look on his face that indicated Glynis had gotten off easy by not having Myrtle teach her English.

"We got along okay. I don't usually live here, of course, so it's not like we spent a lot of time together. I mean, we squabbled a lot growing up, but that's pretty typical, ain't it?" He corrected himself quickly as Myrtle's eyebrows knit together. "Isn't it?"

"She'd invited you to stay with her during your visit to Bradley?" asked Miles. "That was nice."

Edgar blinked at him with surprise, as if he'd forgotten he was there. "Well, you know, it's Christmas and everything. I guess I'm the prodigal brother or something. Even though Glynis was kind of crusty, she was really happy to see me. Took me right into the house and gave me the warmest hug I ever got." He glanced around the palatial home. "I'm thinking about redoing the house, though. Making it more like something I'd like to live in. I'm *definitely* going to put a Christmas wreath on the door. I love the holiday, but Glynis was sort of a grinch."

Myrtle said, "You're planning on staying here?"

"Sure, why not? I like changing things up a little bit. Maybe I'll settle back down here for a while. I could get used to this place." He glanced around him at the tall ceilings and stately furniture.

"Glynis left her house to you?" Myrtle quirked an eyebrow.

Edgar grinned at her. "Well, you can't take it with you, can you? I figure Glynis would have remembered her old brother. She told me once, years ago, she'd make sure to take care of me."

"How *many* years ago?" asked Myrtle.

Edgar had to think about this. "Gosh, it's been a while. Maybe it was even before I had Faith."

Myrtle reflected that a lot could change in the course of twenty-five years.

"Wasn't it a great wedding?" asked Edgar. "What did y'all think?"

Myrtle and Miles made pleasant, agreeing noises.

Edgar continued, "It was like a dream, wasn't it? Faith looked so pretty—just like her mama, she did. Holden seems like a nice young man. I'd say they have a great future together. I'm proud of both of them."

"It was certainly a lovely evening, up until the end," said Myrtle in a rather stern voice. She didn't think it was very appropriate for Edgar to be waxing poetic about the wedding when his own sister had perished during the reception.

Edgar looked grave. "Absolutely. God rest Glynis's soul. Wish I could have been the good brother and stopped it all from happening. As it was, though, I had no idea what was happening. I was busy toasting the bride."

Myrtle, remembering Edgar slumped in his chair, had the feeling that Edgar had toasted the bride quite a few times.

Edgar sighed. "That's the thing, though. I always came across to our folks as the irresponsible kid, compared to Glynis. Maybe it makes sense that I'm the one who was partying instead of looking after my sister when she died. Our parents were always proud of Glynis: her grades, the college she went to, her great job. There was no way I could compare with Glynis." He shrugged. "So I stopped trying."

"Do you have any idea who might have done this to your sister? I know you haven't been living here, but did Glynis confide in you at all?" Myrtle thought this was certainly a longshot. She had the feeling that Glynis so disapproved of Edgar that they weren't in touch at all.

Edgar nodded eagerly. "I bet I can tell you who did it. That smarmy surgeon. Did you know he wasn't supposed to be at the wedding at all? Glynis said she'd uninvited him as soon as she'd dumped him."

"She told you that?" asked Miles with a surprised expression on his face.

Edgar said, "Nope. But I overheard her telling some other people. She said Nash was calling her and dropping by and wouldn't leave her alone after she'd broken up with him. Glynis said something about hating his schedule and how work seemed more important to him than their relationship."

Myrtle said crisply, "I'd think Glynis would have known going in that Nash wouldn't have regular hours. Surgeons don't."

Edgar shrugged. "She said he was the kind of person who was used to getting his own way and he was real unhappy at being dumped. Even though he'd done some dumping of his own, she said."

Myrtle said, "I see. He wasn't used to being scorned. Well, I hope they find the person responsible for Glynis's death soon, Edgar." She stood to indicate the end of the visit and Miles happily rose, too.

Edgar said curiously, "Ain't your son the police chief now?" Seeing Myrtle's unhappy expression, he quickly said, "Isn't he?"

"He is and has been for quite some time. I guess the two of you must have been in school together about the same time."

"I was a few years older than he was, but yeah. You don't happen to know what Red is thinking, do you? About who done it? I mean, did it?"

Myrtle said coolly, "Unfortunately, I never know what Red is thinking, Edgar. And now I believe Miles and I should probably leave. We have a rather busy day."

Edgar nodded and stood up to walk them out. "Gotcha. Well, I thank you both for coming over. And for the food. I'll be eating that for my supper tonight."

Myrtle beamed at him. "I hope you'll enjoy it."

"I'm sure I will."

Miles had a slight smile on his face as they walked out the door.

A minute later, in Miles's car, he asked, "We have a busy day today? What is it we're doing?"

"Well, we have the book club party tonight at Tippy's house."

"That's hours away," said Miles. "Particularly since it's so early that we woke Edgar up from a sound sleep."

Myrtle waved her hand. "He was sleeping hard because of all the beer he drank last night. You saw all the beer cans strewn around the room. That doesn't even count what he drank at the wedding reception. Although I did get the impression that he could probably drink other people under the table. He seemed more of a habitual drinker than not."

"You think he could have murdered Glynis? For money?"

"You've got that distasteful look on your face, Miles. Of course he could have done that. Edgar has nothing, as far as I'm aware. You saw how delighted he was at the prospect of inheriting Glynis's house. But I believe that's just a pipe dream of his. There's absolutely no way that Glynis would have left her beautiful house to her no-good brother."

Miles said, "You think Glynis left her house to Faith?"

"I wouldn't be at all surprised if Glynis left her house to charity instead. She always did exactly what she wanted to do. I'll be very interested to find out. But no—she decidedly didn't leave it to Edgar. She'd have to have had a minor stroke to have done that."

They walked in to see Wanda, who greeted them with a grin. She was playing solitaire while Pasha watched with feline interest.

"How did it go?" asked Wanda.

"Edgar was *delighted* by the casserole. He can't wait to eat it," said Myrtle as she put her purse away.

Wanda and Miles exchanged a glance.

"He's a very bad father," said Miles quietly to Wanda, by means of explaining how he permitted an atrocious casserole to slip by him.

Myrtle continued on blithely, "And we learned that Edgar believes Nash, the surgeon who was dating Glynis, might be responsible for her death. He doesn't know that, of course, but that's his suspicion. Apparently, he was rather unglued by Glynis dumping him."

Wanda frowned, looking thoughtfully into space.

Myrtle caught the frown. "Are you getting some sort of signal about Nash, Wanda?"

Wanda nodded. "Somethin' bad."

"Anything more *helpful* than that?" asked Myrtle.

Miles gave Myrtle a reproving look.

"Naw," said Wanda sadly. "Jest something' bad."

"Never mind, then. I'm sure it will come to you later. Let's get a snack and then work on puzzles. I'd like to work on my crossword. Are you going to tackle the Sudoku, Miles?"

He shook his head. "I'd like to play gin rummy with Wanda."

Wanda, who'd been still looking sad at the mention of Nash, started beaming.

The rest of the morning was quiet, spent with puzzles and cards. Then they had sandwiches and chips and watched *Tomorrow's Promise* in the afternoon as Pasha napped on Wanda's lap. Afterwards, Miles retreated home for a nap.

There was a light tap on the door.

Myrtle opened it to find her yard man, Dusty, standing there, looking grim. Dusty usually looked grim, however.

"Merry Christmas," he said brusquely.

"Merry Christmas to you, Dusty. And I'm delighted to see you. I've been wondering when you were going to come by and pull my gnomes out."

Dusty grunted at this. "Sorta thought you might put the gnomes on hold, seein' as how it's Christmas and everything."

"What? No, of course not. They're actually going to be part of my Christmas display. My gnomes have some fetching Santa hats to wear. And I'll string lights around a few of them."

Dusty looked at Myrtle and her cane with a doubtful expression. "*You'll* be stringin' lights around 'em?"

"I suppose there's not a lot of room to maneuver between them, is there? Very well, I'll have you do that . . . the lights are in the storage shed. But I'll put the Santa hats on the little guys."

Dusty grunted again and stomped off to get the gnomes out.

Myrtle said to Wanda, "At least that's finally taken care of. I was wondering when Dusty would make it over. Now I can concentrate on the rest of the day. You'll go with Miles and me to Tippy's party later, won't you?"

Wanda looked rather alarmed at this. "Wasn't invited."

"It simply doesn't matter, Wanda. You know how all the ladies fawn over you when you're there. They all want to hear your predictions for things."

Wanda looked stubborn. "It's book club. I don't really read."

"Neither do they! Or what they choose to read is very silly stuff. Besides, we didn't have a book for this month because that club finds any excuse not to read. And, believe me, I'm glad. I needed time to recover from the November pick, *The Girl on the Airplane*. It was most nonsensical. If you're seriously uncomfortable, of course you can stay here. But the food will be fabulous, the decorations will be lovely, and it might be fun. I just don't want you to be left out."

Wanda considered this. "Okay." She grinned at Myrtle. "I got somethin' to wear, at least."

"You surely do."

Which is how they were both ready, in their finest clothes, when Miles picked them up at six.

Chapter Seven

Tippy's house was a colonial monstrosity with verandas and columns and lots of windows. She had every bit of the outside decorated with tasteful Christmas decorations. The house was completely lit with yellow lights, there were candles on the window sills and wreaths hanging on every window and door.

Miles gave a low whistle. "It must have taken her forever to decorate."

Myrtle snorted. "Tippy didn't lift a finger. She has decorators to handle everything . . . she told me about it last year."

"That must be nice," said Miles as they walked toward the house.

"I sort of have decorators, too. Dusty puts all my gnomes in place, after all."

Miles's expression seemed to say that he much-preferred Tippy's decorations.

Wanda muttered, "Sounds like a lot of people in there."

"Hmm? Oh, yes. It'll be a much-larger group than it usually is. The women would have brought their husbands with them. And I suppose the single women might have brought a date. So, there will be roughly double the number of people there."

Wanda seemed to be squaring her shoulders as if she might be facing an army.

Myrtle noticed. "And Wanda, we'll find a quiet spot for you to hang out. I won't have people swarming you to get their fortunes; I know how much that depletes your energy. My goal is for you to enjoy people-watching, to eat some delicious food, and to just relax."

Wanda looked a bit doubtful.

"I'm carrying a cane and I'm not afraid to use it," said Myrtle, shaking her cane still strung with the cheerful red ribbon.

The inside of Tippy's house was just as tastefully decorated as the outside. There were cheerful garlands, a tremendous live Christmas tree with all-white ornaments and lights, and stockings hung over a raging fire in the huge fireplace. There was also a coy bit of mistletoe hanging subtly in a doorway.

Tippy was wearing a cocktail dress and loads of diamond jewelry as she walked around greeting her guests. Wanda made a muttering sound.

"It's fine. Tippy always overdresses. You and I look delightful," said Myrtle.

"I would agree," said Miles chivalrously.

"Let's greet Tippy and then find the food," said Myrtle.

Tippy spotted them walking toward her and smiled at them. "What a pleasure to see you all here. And Wanda! I'm so glad you could make it."

Tippy made it sound as if she'd always intended Wanda to be there. But then, Tippy was the perfect hostess.

Wanda colored. "Sorry I jest showed up."

Tippy looked appalled that Wanda would even think that. "What? No. You're *always* invited, Wanda." She frowned. "Perhaps it would be better in future if I mailed an invitation to you."

Wanda shook her head. "Mailbox done fell down. Ain't getting no mail."

"All right then. But promise me that you'll remember there's an implicit invitation for you to come to any of my functions. *Always*."

Wanda nodded shyly and Tippy looked assured of the point. "Excellent. Now why don't the three of you find something to eat? These folks seem very hesitant to be the first to get a plate."

"We'll solve that problem," said Myrtle, who had no patience with guests who wouldn't eat at parties. "We've come hungry."

"Wonderful!" said Tippy. "I don't need any leftovers, so be sure to take food home with you."

Myrtle said, "I can't believe it, but I forgot to bring my plastic container with me. I was too focused on getting dressed and ready."

"Well, you look lovely," said Tippy. And then she subtly gestured to a server to come over. "Could you bring Miss Myrtle a container to put any extra food in? Thank you."

"Thanks, Tippy," said Myrtle.

"The food tables are there, there, and there," said Tippy, pointing out the areas spread over the tremendous first floor. "The punch is over there—there's one that's labeled as non-alcoholic and one that's been gently spiked. Let me know if you need anything."

And she quickly left, just as fast as she'd arrived.

Miles said, "I'm amazed Tippy is serving alcohol."

"She said 'gently spiked.' That may mean it has a tiny bit of low-proof liqueur in it," said Myrtle. "Tippy probably put it out for us since it appears other guests are taking different approaches."

And indeed, Blanche seemed to be drinking from a flask and passing it to Georgia, who grinned and took a gulp.

Miles said glumly, "Well, that's that. We've seen what happens when this group has alcohol."

"Hilarity ensues," said Myrtle with satisfaction. She paused and said, "Look who Blanche brought with her."

Blanche was hanging on the arm of Nash Moore, the surgeon Glynis had dumped just before her sudden demise.

Wanda grunted. "That's gonna be trouble."

"Is it?" asked Myrtle. "What's going to happen?"

"Bad things," said Wanda, somewhat unhelpfully.

Miles said, "Well, we can't stand here staring at them. Let's get our food."

Tippy had gone all out for the book club Christmas party, as usual. There were chaffing dishes full of hot chicken, roast beef, and honey-glazed ham. The sides were vegetables and numerous enough that anyone could have a veggie plate, if they so desired.

Wanda's eyes were huge as they heaped their plates high with food. "This even beats her other parties."

"She has a particular fondness for Christmas," said Myrtle. "Let's bring our food over there. It's a quiet spot and we'll be able to people-watch without any problems."

But there *was* a problem. Erma Sherman suddenly appeared, leering at them and holding a sheaf of papers. "Thought I might see the three of you together. Maybe I'm getting as psychic as Wanda!"

Wanda gave her a polite smile.

Myrtle, on the other hand, shot her a cold look. "Hi Erma."

Erma looked especially pleased with herself. "I knew Tippy had a grand piano."

Miles eyes widened as if he knew what was coming but couldn't look away from the approaching trainwreck.

"I've been practicing Christmas carols on my keyboard at home. I'm going to do a concert!"

Myrtle looked at her askance. "Did you okay this with Tippy?"

Erma gave her braying laugh. "Of course not. It's supposed to be a surprise."

"I'm sure it *will* be a surprise. The only problem is that Tippy is not at all fond of surprises. She's the sort of person who prefers to be in control of all aspects of her parties. Even the . . . music," said Myrtle.

Erma snorted. "Well, she doesn't even *have* music playing right now, so it shouldn't be a problem." She whirled around, sheet music in hand.

Miles watched with concern as Erma lumbered toward the grand piano. "Do you think she knows how to play?"

"Of course she doesn't know how to play. The very idea is completely ridiculous."

Wanda winced in advance of the performance.

Erma plopped down on the piano bench with a flounce. Then she started hitting keys. The resulting cacophony was truly terrible.

"I can't even tell what Christmas carol this is," muttered Myrtle.

Miles said, "Maybe we should head outside onto Tippy's patio."

"No, because now there's an exodus outdoors, and we might get trampled in the process of trying to escape. Surely someone will persuade her to stop."

"She can't believe this music is any good," said Miles.

"Yes, she can," drawled Wanda.

Myrtle said, "Oh, good. Georgia is heading over to the piano. She can be rather frightening. Maybe she'll stop Erma."

But Georgia apparently had no intention of stopping Erma. "Christmas carols!" bellowed Georgia. "Great idea!"

"She's *encouraging* her," said Miles in horror.

Myrtle pursed her lips. "She's clearly been drinking far too much."

"Bad things happen when this group drinks," said Miles sadly.

Georgia was peering over Erma's shoulder at the sheet music. "Jingle Bells! I know that one."

And Georgia proceeded to make a bad situation even worse by belting out the song at the top of her lungs.

"She actually has a decent voice," mused Myrtle. "But she's not helping." She noticed that more people were hastily pulling flasks out of their purses and pockets.

Tippy, wringing her hands, slid over to them. "This is a problem," she said in a somber voice. "I don't want to embarrass Erma, though. What can we do?"

Miles squared his shoulders and took a deep breath. "I could play. I could ask Erma as a special favor. Say that it will bring back happy memories from my youth."

Tippy's eyes lit up. "Would you? Oh, that would be wonderful, Miles. You'd be a real hero."

Miles trudged over to the piano and Georgia, halting her enthusiastic rendition of Jingle Bells, greeted him enthusiastically. Erma said loudly, "Trying to horn in, Miles? Okay, you can have a spin."

Miles took Erma's place at the piano and began to play *God Rest Ye Merry, Gentlemen.*

Wanda smiled.

Myrtle gasped. "For heaven's sake. He can really play."

Miles's piano music was so good that people stopped their conversations to just listen to him. He played several carols in a row and then stopped, giving his audience a shy smile. The audience, in return, burst into energetic applause. He gave a little bow and then joined Myrtle and Wanda.

"Look," said Myrtle. "You were so good that Erma doesn't want to play now. Well done, Miles!" And then, in a low voice, "I think you have a fan coming your way. Nash Moore."

The surgeon came up and patted Miles on the back. "Many thanks. You've saved the book club party from a horrible death.

I'm Nash Moore." He shook Miles's hand and then offered his hand to Wanda with a slightly confused look on his face. "And I'm not sure we've met either, ma'am."

Wanda looked a bit flustered at being called ma'am. "Wanda," she mumbled.

"And Miss Myrtle, of course I know you." He gave her a big smile.

"Nash was one of my most excellent students," Myrtle told the others. "It's easy enough to be smart. *Plenty* of kids are smart. But to be smart, try hard, and be organized is a very effective combination. I'm never surprised how far you went."

He gave her a rueful look. "Apparently I liked school so much that I chose to go for a couple of decades. Good seeing you here."

Myrtle raised an eyebrow. "I believe you're here with my friend, Blanche?"

Nash nodded. "That's right. We've just recently started seeing each other."

"She's a lot of fun, I suppose."

They looked over at Blanche who, having had quite a few sips from her own flask, was raucously laughing at something Tippy had said. Tippy gave her guest a rather alarmed look.

"She is," said Nash, although his smile was somewhat forced.

"I believe you might have previously been seeing Glynis?" asked Myrtle. "I'm sorry for your loss."

"Nothing ever did make it past you, Miss Myrtle. You're right—Glynis and I were dating for a long while. I was very satisfied with that arrangement, although Glynis apparently wasn't. She ended our relationship not long before she died."

Nash looked conflicted for a moment and then said, "Actually, Miss Myrtle, I've been wanting to talk to you for a little while. About Red." He paused. "Perhaps we should step out onto the patio and speak in private?"

Wanda and Miles started to move away but Myrtle said sharply, "Certainly not. Whatever you say to me can be said in front of my friends."

Nash took a deep breath. "Okay. I just feel as if your son has been asking a lot of really objectionable questions."

"I'm not at all surprised. Red is completely impossible."

Nash looked surprised that Myrtle was siding with him. Encouraged, he continued, "Of *course* I didn't murder Glynis. I cared a lot for her and was trying to get her to come back to me. She was so intelligent—really, she was an academic. We had like minds."

Blanche was, sadly, singing now. Fortunately, others were joining in and masking her rather objectionable voice.

Nash winced and said, "Of course, life must go on. The fact I'm here with Blanche doesn't mean my feelings for Glynis are finished. And, as I told Red, I'm in the business of saving lives, not eliminating them."

There was pride on his face as he talked about his job. Myrtle supposed that, like many surgeons, he had something of a God complex.

"Basically, I had nothing to do with Glynis's death. I wasn't even at the wedding reception."

Wanda gave a small, slow shake of her head.

Myrtle said crisply, "You must think I'm a dotty old lady, Nash."

Nash, perhaps remembering Myrtle's sharp tongue, said quickly, "Not at all. Your mind is as agile as ever."

"I know you were at the wedding reception. I saw you there, with my own eyes. I've heard others mention you were there, as well. I can't imagine you were invited. If you were, then your invitation must surely have been rescinded."

Nash turned an unattractive shade of purple. "I was only there for a few minutes before I reconsidered and left for home. In fact, I spotted Glynis heading off for a cigarette when I was leaving in the other direction." He shook his head. "A nasty habit, smoking. I kept telling her cigarettes were going to be the end of her. And, in a way, I suppose they were."

"If you were leaving, I suppose you could have trotted around and murdered her and then headed on your way," said Myrtle thoughtfully.

Nash's eyes were huge and he appeared to be trying to calm himself down. Myrtle had the distinct impression that he was not accustomed to being questioned. He gave her a twisted smile. "Now I see where Red got his propensity for questioning everything."

Myrtle gave him a demure smile. "I'm not saying you *did* it, Nash. I'm just saying you don't really have an alibi. A fact I'm sure my son has glommed onto."

Nash said stiffly, "As I was saying, I enjoyed my relationship with Glynis and, in fact, wanted it to continue. It wouldn't have made sense for me to have murdered her. We spent hours talking to each other about books, movies, and music. I was under the apparently mistaken impression that we were soulmates. In fact, I ended the relationship I was in to date Glynis."

Myrtle said, "Who were you dating before?"

Nash was starting to look as if he regretted coming over to speak with them. He said, "Belinda Clark."

Myrtle was sure she'd heard that name mentioned to her recently, but she couldn't quite figure out when. "How did Belinda feel about your dating Glynis?"

Nash shrugged. "She wasn't happy about it, of course. In fact, she was furious. I can't believe how she changed overnight. When I ended our relationship, she started pestering both Glynis and me. Glynis had to block her number because she was spamming her so much. She really lost it. I think she's simply spoiled and used to getting her own way."

Myrtle figured it took one to know one. "Do you think Belinda could possibly have it in her to be violent?"

Nash vigorously nodded. "Could you tell Red that? I didn't even think about mentioning Belinda to him. Maybe it will give me a break from being a suspect. Besides, Red's attention could really besmirch my reputation. Patients want a surgeon they can trust."

Myrtle said smoothly, "Of course I'll pass the information along to Red."

She had absolutely no intention of doing so.

Nash was about to further petition his cause when Blanche, a bit tipsy, ran up, grabbed Nash by the arm, and propelled him under the modest clump of mistletoe.

Miles looked about as uncomfortable at the potential for a public display of affection as Nash did.

"Just turn away, Miles, if it bothers you," said Myrtle. "Although you watch so many soap operas that you should be immune to it."

Miles flushed. "That's not supposed to be public knowledge, Myrtle."

"I won't tell a single soul."

Myrtle glanced over at Wanda's empty plate. "Would you like a second helping?"

"I'll get another plate of food for you," said Miles in the manner of someone happy for something to do.

Myrtle said to Wanda, "What did you make of Nash?"

"He's lying," she croaked.

"Is he? Did the Sight tell you that?"

Wanda shook her head. "Didn't need no Sight to know he was lying."

"Very true," said Myrtle thoughtfully. "That was my impression, too. He was even caught out in one of the lies—that he hadn't been at the wedding reception. If he was willing to give a brazen lie like that, he might be willing to lie about just about anything."

Miles returned with the food, and Wanda happily busied herself with eating. Myrtle and Miles watched the guests, who were getting increasingly loud and boisterous as the evening progressed. Georgia was now singing Christmas carols solo and Myrtle was quite concerned Erma might decide she needed to accompany her. Tippy's face held an expression of great vexation.

Myrtle smiled. "The annual book club Christmas party is an entertaining tradition, isn't it, Miles?"

She reached out her glass of minimally spiked punch and he clinked his glass against it.

Chapter Eight

Later, Miles dropped them off at home. Wanda was full from all the food and happily stumbled off to bed for an early night. Myrtle read for a little while. She'd decided to pick up Christmas books at the library and had a very satisfying collection. She'd already read some of the short stories in one book, including a re-read of O. Henry's *The Gift of the Magi*, Twain's *A Letter from Santa Claus*, and Hans Christian Anderson's *The Little Match Girl*. Now she was settling into Dickens for the grand finale with *A Christmas Carol*.

Curled up with the book, she heard a scratching at the door.

"Dear Pasha," she murmured, going to open it.

Pasha swiftly entered, throwing a furtive look behind her.

"Was there someone out there?" asked Myrtle with a frown.

Pasha looked backwards indignantly, prompting Myrtle to step outside into her yard.

She blinked in the bright lights. Some of the lights were spotlight-type snowflakes that swirled on Erma's house. There was a huge inflatable Santa with spotlights shining on him. Red, green, and blue lights twinkled and blinked on Erma's roofline and throughout her yard.

Myrtle gazed at the ghastly display in horror.

It was then, belatedly, she noticed Erma standing to the side, admiring her handiwork. Unfortunately, Erma had already spotted her and sprinted over, a grin on her donkey-like features.

"What do you think?" she asked excitedly.

Myrtle, speechless for once, shook her head.

"Isn't it great? I put the lights up earlier today and realized I hadn't set up the timer before Tippy's party, so I went ahead and turned it on."

Myrtle stared again at the light show.

"Oh, you're probably wondering about the lights on the roof. Yep, I even did those myself! I'm pretty coordinated, though. I don't think *you* should do it." She gave a raucous laugh as she looked at the cane Myrtle held in one hand.

Myrtle subdued the fleeting, overwhelming instinct to whack Erma with the cane.

"Well, I'll talk to you tomorrow. Merry Christmas, Myrtle!"

With that, Erma sprinted back to further revere her creation as Myrtle walked slowly back inside.

Pasha gave her a sympathetic look as she entered the house. Myrtle plopped on the sofa and reached for the black cat. Pasha jumped next to her and leaned against Myrtle.

"It's awful, that's what it is," muttered Myrtle. "It's quite late to put up such a display, too, which makes me think she's going to have the things up until February, at the very least. Plus, I have the sneaking suspicion those horrid lights are going to keep me awake tonight."

Soon, it was time to test her theory. After she'd let Pasha back out into the darkness again, she turned in. Sure enough, multi-colored lights moved in circular patterns on her walls, despite the blinds being pulled. Myrtle groaned in annoyance.

After a restless night, Myrtle finally managed to fall asleep around four. This time, it was she who woke up with the smell of breakfast cooking. She noticed with amazement that her bedside clock reported it was nearly eight o'clock.

"Mercy!" said Myrtle. It felt as if it were the middle of the day. She slid her feet into her favorite slippers and pulled on her bathrobe.

Wanda grinned at her from the kitchen. "Got you some eggs and bacon this mornin'."

"I'm surprised you didn't come into my room to check for a pulse. I don't think I've slept this late for decades."

Wanda chuckled. "Heard you snorin' so figured you was okay."

Myrtle rubbed her eyes. "I feel groggy. It's like I have a sleep hangover. Did you have a problem sleeping last night with those horrid lights?"

"That Erma?" asked Wanda. "Them was pretty."

Different strokes for different folks, figured Myrtle. She sighed. "Unfortunately, they're the sort of lights guaranteed to keep me awake. Bright. Twinkling. Mobile."

Wanda grimaced. "Sorry 'bout that. Maybe some coffee will help?"

Myrtle found that Wanda could make an excellent pot of coffee. Her breakfast-making skills, as she'd discovered before, were also superb. And she did indeed feel better now that she had a bit of caffeine and some food.

"Whatcha plannin' on doin' today?" asked Wanda in-between bites of food.

"Oh, I suppose I'll see where the day leads me." Myrtle paused. "I did pick up some intel last night at Tippy's party. Did you overhear Blanche talking about a cookie swap?"

Wanda gave her a wry look. "Couldn't help but hear it. She was yellin' by that time."

"True. I've noticed before that alcohol and Blanche are not a good combination. Anyway, there's some sort of secret cookie swap party underfoot. I'm quite peeved I haven't been invited." Myrtle pursed her lips.

"What's a cookie swap?"

"Oh, it's an excuse for a party. Everyone makes their favorite cookies. Lots of cookies. Then the guests all bring home different types of Christmas cookies. Oh, and you share the recipe too, I guess. Anyway, I've noticed that I simply do not ever get invites for those cookie swapping parties. It's because everyone assumes older people are watching their sugar intake and so forth."

Wanda gave her a somewhat skeptical look but nodded in agreement.

"So one of the things I should do today is find out precisely when and where the cookie swap is so that I can be prepared."

Wanda asked, "Gonna crash the party?"

"Absolutely. Octogenarians get away with everything."

After they'd cleaned up the kitchen, Myrtle's phone rang. She frowned, peering at it. "Goodness. It's Elaine. She's calling early."

"Prob'ly thinks you've been up for five or six hours," drawled Wanda.

Myrtle picked up the phone. "Elaine? Is everything all right?"

It was a valid question, since there was wailing going on in the background on Elaine's end.

"Oh, it's just morning," said Elaine wryly. "Jack is upset because he knocked his sippy cup off his table for the millionth time, and I won't pick it up again. Sorry to call you about this, but I wondered if you could help me out today."

There was nothing Myrtle liked better than helping Elaine out. It was always good to be useful. "Of course."

Elaine chuckled. "You might want to hear what it is first before you agree. I need Teacher Myrtle today."

"And Teacher Myrtle is happy to comply. Where should I report for my teaching assignment?"

"The church. You'll remember I'm the director of the Christmas pageant?" asked Elaine.

Myrtle did remember. At the time, she had the sinking feeling the pageant would likely end up as Elaine's other pursuits often did—not going particularly well.

Elaine continued, "I've been having a really tough time, I'll admit. Belinda Clark is an assistant director, but she's about as hopeless as I am in maintaining control."

"Control? I understood these were preschoolers and kindergartners."

Elaine sighed. "That's right. But they're like herding cats. I especially need extra help wrangling shepherds. I'll be trying to coach the angels on their lines and the shepherds will be running around like wild things, whooping and hollering. You have such a commanding presence and great teacher voice that I immediately thought of you. It's a pretty important practice today—we're essentially supposed to be ready for the play by the end of it."

"I see. Of course I'll be there. What time?"

Elaine told Myrtle when she'd pick her up and then said with another gusty sigh, "I should go now."

According to the screaming on the other end of the line, Myrtle agreed. She hung up the phone thoughtfully.

"Trouble?" asked Wanda.

Myrtle nodded. "Elaine is trying something new again. And apparently, she's not particularly adept at corralling children. I'm to lend my teaching voice to the chaos."

Wanda raised an eyebrow.

"I know," said Myrtle. "But, on the upside, I'll have the opportunity to speak with Belinda Clark. She's the one who dated Nash Moore before he started dating Glynis. I wasn't sure how I was going to manage a conversation with Belinda—this sort of fell in my lap."

"Want me to help?"

Myrtle appreciated the offer but saw Wanda looked particularly anxious. She didn't have much experience with children. "Not a bit. You should hang out and relax. I think you might enjoy the morning game shows since you enjoy cards and games."

Wanda gave her a relieved smile.

An hour later, Myrtle climbed into Elaine's minivan. She turned to look at Jack in the backseat and he grinned at her. "Hi, Nana."

"Hi there, Jack! What a wonderful boy you're being." She gave Elaine a sideways look.

Elaine gave her a rueful look. "Whenever you happen to see him, he's a perfect angel. I swear he's not always like that."

"Of course he is! Aren't you, Jack?"

Jack smiled conspiratorially at his grandmother.

"Who's Jack going to be in the play?" asked Myrtle. "The baby Jesus?"

Elaine snorted. "No, Myrtle. Despite what you might think, Jack isn't quite *that* good. A baby doll is playing the role of baby Jesus. Jack is going to be a lamb."

"A *lamb*? And his mother's the director of the play? I should think he'd land a bigger part than *that*."

Elaine shrugged a shoulder. "He makes an excellent lamb, actually."

"Isn't this the dress rehearsal? He doesn't appear to have a costume on."

Elaine said, "Well, he's not crazy about the costume. I'll put it on him about halfway through the practice."

They arrived at the church and walked into the church hall. There was already a motley assortment of angels, shepherds, wise men, and sheep there. As soon as the parents spotted Elaine, they told their little ones goodbye and quickly fled.

"Where is Belinda?" asked Myrtle.

"She usually wanders in a few minutes late. She's nice, but she worries a lot about the children's feelings and less about the chaos."

Myrtle asked, "Belinda has children?"

"She has a child from her first marriage."

As Elaine spoke, the chaos immediately ensued. Shepherds and wise men were chasing each other while tripping over their own costumes. The angels were playing a game on one of the mother's phones, which had apparently been accidentally left behind. Nobody seemed to pay any attention, as Elaine called the group to order.

Myrtle spotted Belinda coming in with her daughter. She was also on her phone and didn't seem in any hurry to help.

Myrtle reached out and flipped the lights off.

Suddenly, there was complete and total silence.

Myrtle turned them on and gave a piercing look to each and every one of the assorted cast members. "Children? Here's what you're going to do. Sit in a big circle and listen. Your director is going to tell you what to do next. The better you listen, the better this practice is going to go."

Elaine gave Myrtle a grateful look and Myrtle bobbed her head.

The children, recognizing authority despite its unlikely source, settled into a lopsided circle and kept a watchful eye on Myrtle.

The practice proceeded to go extremely well. Anytime things threatened to become disorderly, Myrtle reached a hand toward the light switch and chaos was averted. She also found that a simple shake of the head discouraged a couple of the shepherds from trying to wrestle with each other. At the end of the hour, the practice appeared to be a success. And Jack made an absolutely adorable lamb.

"The star of the show," muttered Myrtle, still irritated that he wasn't recognized as such with a starring role.

Elaine was chatting with the mothers who were picking up their children, and Belinda came over to speak with Myrtle for a few minutes. She was holding her daughter, who smiled shyly at Myrtle.

Myrtle smiled back at the little girl and then at Belinda.

Belinda said, "I have to thank you. I was really dreading coming here today, you know. The previous practices have been total and complete nightmares. The kids would run all over the room playing chase and Elaine and I couldn't seem to get things under control. You were amazing."

Myrtle beamed at her. "You just need to establish who's in charge, that's all."

Belinda said ruefully, "I was worried more about embarrassing a child by calling them out for their behavior."

"You get over that when you teach. Usually a stare will suffice."

Belinda snorted. "If you say so. I guess I was never destined to be a teacher."

Myrtle, wanting to get onto the subject of murder, quickly diverted the subject. "Well, it was actually a delight to be here today. I was glad to get a sneak preview of the play. It was such a lovely distraction from all the terrible things going on right now."

Belinda looked grim at the mention of terrible things. "I can't say I'll miss Glynis, although she certainly didn't deserve what happened to her."

Myrtle didn't think Belinda sounded too convinced of that.

Belinda continued, "I didn't go to the wedding, of course, but I heard what happened and feel terrible for Faith. What an awful thing to happen." She put down her daughter and the little girl ran off to see a friend. Belinda absently watched her go.

Myrtle said, "Oh, I didn't realize you knew Glynis."

"I knew her all right. I was dating Nash Moore when she stole him from me." Belinda's voice was bitter.

"I'm acquainted with Nash. I didn't realize the two of you had been seeing each other," said Myrtle, knowing perfectly well they had.

Belinda nodded. "We were going to get married."

Chapter Nine

Myrtle's eyebrows shot up. This was news indeed. "Were you? You were engaged?"

"Nash hadn't asked me yet, but it was only a matter of time. We'd been dating for years. He was going to pop the question anytime."

Myrtle wasn't altogether sure that was inevitable. "And you say Glynis stole him from you?"

Belinda's face flushed. "She knew Nash and I were seeing each other and that it was serious. I don't think she was really even interested in Nash, not really. But Glynis was the kind of person who, when faced with a challenge, would try to meet it. So she flirted and flaunted her money and called him up and pretty soon, he fell for it."

"But you say Glynis wasn't all that into Nash?"

Belinda shook her head. "Nope. That's completely obvious from the way she dumped him later."

"Why did she do that?"

"Because the two of them had nothing in common," said Belinda, waving her hands in the air with some agitation.

Elaine and a couple of the moms eyed Belinda's hand-waving with interest, possibly wondering why her conversation with the octogenarian was becoming so animated.

"You must have been furious with Glynis," said Myrtle, trying to make it sound like an innocent statement.

But Belinda immediately realized she was treading into dangerous waters. She carefully said, "I was angrier with Nash than I was with Glynis. He betrayed me and Glynis was simply doing what came naturally to her. I really harbored no ill feelings toward Glynis."

"That was very generous of you."

Belinda shrugged. "I mean, for a while I'd cross to the other side of the street when I spotted Glynis coming. But then I decided that I'd do the adult thing and just try to get over it. Although I'd originally wanted Nash back at any cost, I finally realized that it wasn't really meant to be."

Myrtle nodded. "If he was going to be the kind of man who has a wandering eye, it was better to know before the relationship became a marriage."

"Exactly," said Belinda. But it sounded to Myrtle as if she was trying to convince herself of that fact. "Anyway, I think my anger is now centered more where it *should* be . . . with Nash. He betrayed me and I'm not the kind of person who takes that lightly. I was betrayed by my first husband, so I'm particularly sensitive to it."

Jack came running up to Myrtle, still in his adorable lamb costume. She beamed at him and said, "See? Your costume isn't so bad, is it? But now it's time to take it off."

She helped him out of the costume and then reached into her purse. "Would you like a candy cane?"

Jack's eyes grew big, and he nodded.

Myrtle unwrapped the candy cane and said, "Now, you'll need to sit on the floor to eat this. We don't want to run around and choke."

Jack obediently plopped to the floor and held out his hand for the candy cane.

Myrtle smiled at Jack and then turned back to Belinda. "Sorry about that. You were talking about Nash, I believe."

Belinda said ruefully, "About my disastrous love life. Yes, my first husband was a rogue, too. He ended up leaving me for someone ten years younger. After that, I guess I have trouble trusting people. Then I ended up with Nash, and he really reinforced that I can't trust people."

"I think there are folks out there that you *can* trust. You probably just need to think outside the box in terms of whom you date."

Belinda looked as if this was a completely new and revolutionary idea. "I think you might be right. I have this pattern of dating the same kind of guy. It's always the same type."

"Handsome surgeons?" Myrtle raised her eyebrow.

"Handsome and successful men, I guess. Men with big egos. I'll have to work on that." Belinda sighed a little, as if it wasn't going to be easy to do so. "And now I think I should collect my daughter and head out. Thanks again for your help today, Miss Myrtle."

Belinda left to collect her daughter, and Myrtle looked down at Jack. He was, she discovered, completely covered in sticky candy cane. Somehow, it was even up in his hair. He looked very happy, though, as he took the last bite of the little cane.

Myrtle asked him, "Was it good?"

Jack grinned at her.

"Want to go get cleaned up? I think there's a paper towel with your name on it."

Jack nodded, perhaps realizing that stickiness wasn't particularly fun on one's face and hair.

Myrtle waved to Elaine to indicate she had Jack. Then she headed off to the ladies' room. Once there, she ran the water until it was hot and then covered a wad of paper towels with it. As she was working on Jack's face, she could overhear a rather loud conversation taking place outside the restroom. Since she could only hear one end of it, it seemed to be a phone conversation.

"That sounds like Abigail Davis," Myrtle told Jack.

Jack, who thought everything Myrtle said was wonderful, grinned at her again.

The woman on the phone outside said, "Yes, he was most upset at getting called out like that at the wedding reception. Who can blame him? It was a revolting thing to do. But what else could you expect from Glynis?"

Myrtle finished up her handiwork with Jack's hair and added, "She's Holden's aunt. The groom at the fateful wedding I attended. Perhaps we should speak with her, Jack. She might be able to offer us some helpful information."

Jack seemed pleased to be included. They walked out of the restroom just as Abigail was getting off the phone.

Abigail was in her late-fifties and was very involved in volunteering at the church. Myrtle had always found her something of an annoying busybody.

When she saw Jack, her eyes lit up. "Who is this handsome fellow, Miss Myrtle?"

Myrtle found herself feeling a bit more kindly toward Abigail then. "My grandson, Jack."

Abigail stooped and rummaged in her purse for a miniature candy cane. "Look what I have."

Jack's eyes lit up. Myrtle said, "Jack, we'd probably better have that a little later since we just cleaned you up. Can you keep it in a safe place for me?"

Jack held the candy reverently in his small hands.

"What are you doing here today?" asked Abigail curiously. "I don't think I've seen you at the church for a while."

Myrtle pressed her lips together. A busybody, just as she'd always been. Myrtle did want some information from her, though, so she said carelessly, "Oh, I was just helping with the Christmas pageant practice. That sort of thing."

Abigail's eyes grew wide. "That's a huge job. Are you in charge of the play?"

"I was today." Which was the absolute truth.

Abigail nodded, looking a bit more respectful. "I'm just here to polish the bowl that goes in the baptismal font. There's to be a baptism on Sunday." She looked down at Jack with a smile. "I just love seeing all the young people in the church. I volunteer in the church nursery as often as I can."

Myrtle said, "Yes, children are so sweet." However, Myrtle didn't really feel that way. She thought *Jack* a most remarkable child. Myrtle very much enjoyed the company of *some* children, just as she enjoyed the company of *some* adults. She moved on hastily, "I wanted to tell you how lovely Holden's wedding to Faith was. And the reception was delightful, as well."

Abigail frowned. "The reception? Did you have your hearing aids turned up all the way, my dear?"

Myrtle said icily, "My hearing is perfect."

"Of course it is. Sorry, it's just that some things . . . happened . . . at the reception. I wasn't sure if you perhaps didn't hear them. Or maybe you left early since it was a late night."

"I stay up *quite* late on a regular basis. I know all about Glynis's untimely demise. As a matter of fact, I was the one who discovered poor Glynis." Myrtle's feelings were smarting now from Abigail's careless words about hearing aids and appropriate bedtimes for octogenarians.

Abigail's eyes opened wide. "Mercy! Did you? I certainly didn't know that. What a terrible thing. Of course, Glynis behaved atrociously at the reception, but she certainly didn't deserve to die. I suppose you heard what Glynis was saying? All that nonsense about Holden being lazy and after Faith for Glynis's money?"

Myrtle nodded stiffly.

Abigail sighed. "Holden is truly a wonderful boy. He's always kind to me and so polite and respectful. Sometimes he comes by and does yardwork for me without my even asking. I'm not sure why Glynis never seemed to warm to him. I told Holden that said more about Glynis than it did about him."

Myrtle said, "I know my friend Miles plays chess with Holden. Miles was invited to the wedding as Holden's guest."

"Exactly! See what I mean? How could anyone think someone who plays chess with old folks is no-good? Plus, he works so very hard. He was promoted at the pest control company he works at."

Myrtle said, "He sounds like he's a very hard-working young man." She looked down at Jack who had been watching Abigail's animated waves of her hands with interest. "Well, I should be going. Jack and I have things to do today."

Abigail gave Jack a toothy grin. "Hope you enjoy your candy later."

Myrtle and Jack walked back into the church hall. Elaine spotted them and quickly wrapped up her conversation with one of the other moms to join them. "Ready to go?" she asked brightly.

The three of them walked out to the car together; Myrtle with her cane, Jack skipping, and Elaine weighed down with quite a few tote bags of Christmas play paraphernalia.

As Elaine drove, she looked curiously at Myrtle. "You seemed to be having quite the conversation with Belinda."

"She was very interesting to speak with," said Myrtle. "I don't suppose Red has mentioned her in conjunction with the case, has he?"

Elaine's eyes widened. "No. Why—is she a suspect?" Her expression indicated that she didn't particularly want her play's assistant director to be a murder suspect.

"Well, *I* think she is. She was dating Nash Moore, you see."

Elaine looked confused. "The surgeon? What does he have to do with it?"

"I forget that you've been out of the loop lately."

Elaine laughed. "I've been in the loop, but not when it pertains to murder. I'm all caught up in the preschool circles on local news. But it mostly relates to top preschool programs, educational toys, and how to get preschoolers to eat more vegetables by sneaking them into other foods."

"Which makes complete sense and demonstrates once again that you're an excellent mother. Here's the thing—Nash Moore dumped Belinda in order to date Glynis. Then Glynis dumped Nash Moore. So not only is Belinda a suspect because she was apparently very angry at Glynis, but her ex-boyfriend is a suspect because he might have been upset at Glynis for breaking up with him."

Elaine gave a low whistle, which Jack immediately tried and failed to emulate. "Wow. Actually, you're right. I can't believe I haven't heard about all this. What did Belinda say about it all?"

"She didn't confess to murder, so I think your Christmas pageant is in good shape so far. Belinda claimed that she wasn't really that upset with Glynis. She was mostly angry with Nash for his callous treatment of her."

Elaine said, "I can imagine she was mad at him. From what Belinda told me about her first marriage, it sounds like her husband cheated on her regularly until she divorced him. Just awful."

Myrtle heard some crinkling of plastic and turned to find that Jack's patience with waiting for his candy cane had run out. He gave her a big grin that demonstrated the red part of the candy's stripes had transferred itself all over his mouth.

Elaine swiftly turned and sighed. "Guess we'll be doing some cleaning up back at home."

"A treat from Abigail Davis. She was in the back doing some volunteering," said Myrtle.

Elaine pulled up the minivan in front of Myrtle's house.

"Gnomes!" chirped Jack from the backseat.

Myrtle turned to beam at him. "Brilliant boy. They're all decorated for Christmas, too, aren't they."

"The ones with the Santa hats are the best," said Elaine.

Myrtle smirked. "What does Red think of my holiday display?"

"He finds them very fetching," said Elaine with a chuckle.

Myrtle said, "Better than that unholy disaster taking place next door to me."

"Erma's lights are a bit much. I was worried when I saw them being set up, actually. I had the feeling they were going to be pretty bad."

"I had snowflakes dancing on my bedroom wall all night," grumbled Myrtle. "The very least she could do is to keep her nonsense on her side of the fence."

Elaine's expression seemed to indicate that she wasn't sure how Erma was to confine light to a particular boundary. But she sympathetically nodded her head.

Myrtle got out of the van and walked into her house, waving several times at Jack, who lifted a sticky hand in reply.

Once inside, she was about to close her door when a flash of black fur passed by her.

"Pasha!" she said in a pleased voice.

Pasha gave her an intent look and dropped a live mouse on the floor.

Chapter Ten

Myrtle's eyes grew big. "Pasha, I thought we'd decided you didn't need to perform "The Twelve Days of Christmas."

The mouse scampered off, terrified, into the house.

"Oh dear."

Pasha looked grimly at Myrtle.

"I know. You wanted me to kill the mouse. Or eat it live. I'm not entirely sure what you wanted, but the Christmas presents need to cease and desist, Pasha."

Suddenly Myrtle brightened. "I just remembered. Holden is an exterminator. That's the perfect way for me to have an excuse to speak with him."

She beamed at Pasha and Pasha gave her a feline smile as if the excuse were her plan all along.

Myrtle called the extermination company. It was easy to know which one Holden worked for, because there was only one in town. And she knew Holden would be working because he and Faith were putting their honeymoon off until Christmas, when both their workplaces would be closed.

The woman who answered said they'd send someone out in an hour.

"Will it be Holden Davis?" asked Myrtle. "He's a friend." Of sorts, finished Myrtle silently.

"Yes, he's the one who has the open slot this afternoon," said the woman briskly.

Myrtle hung up, smiling.

Sure enough, an hour later, Holden appeared. "Hi, Miss Myrtle. I hear you have a mouse problem?" He looked doubtfully at the tidy surroundings.

"I do indeed. Pasha, she's my feral cat, has been bringing me live gifts the last few days. I believe she may be enacting 'The Twelve Days of Christmas.'"

Holden looked even more doubtful about that idea. "Well, I'll take care of it for you. You don't have to worry about that."

"Excellent. My first thought had been to let Pasha handle it herself. But she seems determined that I personally manage the gifts she brings me. Besides, the poor mouse would have come to a gory end, and it displayed some courage and ingenuity to get away from Pasha to begin with."

Holden said slowly, "So you're wanting a humane catch-and-release then?"

"Yes. We must show some humanity from time to time, mustn't we? I feel for the little mouse, but just the same, I don't want the creature residing in my house. Clement Clarke Moore must have never dealt with insomnia or mice."

Holden frowned in confusion at this apparent non sequitur.

"The poet who wrote 'A Visit from St. Nicolas.'"

Holden's frown deepened.

Myrtle bit back a sigh. "You know. *Not a creature was stirring, not even a mouse.*"

"Yes!" said Holden, relieved to understand his elderly customer. "Well, I have a little plastic trap and will bait it with cheese."

"Then do you have time for a small chat?" asked Myrtle in her best tremulous old-lady voice. "It's just that I get lonely, you know. It's nice to visit with the young people."

Holden smiled at her. "I do have some extra time this afternoon. I'd love to chat."

Holden set about putting out the little trap for the mouse. Then he joined Myrtle in the living room, where she had already poured him a glass of lemonade.

"How is married life?" asked Myrtle as she handed him the glass.

Holden said, "Well, we're getting used to it. Of course, it hasn't been quite the way we thought we were going to start out. You know, considering what happened to Glynis."

Myrtle nodded. "Yes, that was quite awful. I'm so sorry."

Holden gave her a tired smile. "Thank you."

He looked uncomfortable and Myrtle wondered if that was because Glynis had been so ugly to him at the wedding reception. She asked, "Have the police made any headway in finding the person responsible?"

"I was about to ask you the same thing. Considering the chief is your son."

Myrtle said, "Sadly, Red doesn't share that sort of information with me. I heard you mention that the wedding wasn't videotaped."

Holden shook his head. "Glynis didn't want to spring for that. We had a friend do some videoing on their phone, but it wasn't complete. The police took the video, but I understood that it wasn't helpful to them at all. I mean, I get it . . . why Glynis wouldn't pay for the videography. She'd already put out a lot of money for the rest of the wedding. It's sort of ironic that the thing she didn't want to pay for is the thing that might have found her murderer."

"It sounds as though Glynis had precise ideas as to how she wanted the wedding to run."

Holden sighed. "Yeah. I mean, we were grateful that she paid, but it was tough not to have things the way we wanted them to be."

Myrtle said, "I hope you don't mind my mentioning it, but there was something of a contretemps at the reception."

Holden looked baffled.

"A brouhaha," elaborated Myrtle.

He looked even more bewildered.

Myrtle bit back a sigh. "Glynis seemed unhappy with you."

Holden's features cleared. "Oh, you mean when she yelled out that I was basically good-for-nothing. Yes, that was bad. But Glynis's feelings for me were pretty well-known. I think she told just about everybody about them. You'd think she'd have been happy that I was working an honest job with honest wages."

"But she wasn't?"

"No," said Holden. "She'd apparently expected Faith to marry a doctor or a lawyer or somebody."

"That must have really annoyed you."

Holden shrugged. "Not really. It was a little hurtful, but it wasn't something to get worked up about. I never cared what Glynis thought about my job. But it bothered me that she was so worked up during the reception. Faith had wanted this perfect, happy event, and I was upset when she didn't have it."

"I was surprised Glynis ranted like that during the reception she'd paid for. It was almost as if she were deliberately sabotaging it. Besides, I'd think she'd have wanted to ensure Faith had the pleasant reception she'd wanted. Did Glynis and Faith get along well?"

Holden said, "Faith gets along with everybody. The problem was always Glynis. She just wasn't a warm person . . . not to Faith or to anybody else. It was great she took her in and everything, but from what Faith has said, Glynis expected her to be a little adult from day one. Like she wasn't a child at all. Faith always tried to do exactly what Glynis wanted, but she never really seemed to be able to satisfy her."

"So an outburst like the one at the wedding was normal for Glynis?" asked Myrtle.

"Not really. I think she had too much to drink."

Myrtle raised her eyebrows. "Did she drink too much?"

"Maybe. She wasn't a sloppy drunk, so it was hard to tell. It was never like she was falling all over herself or slurring her words. But she could get harsher when she was drinking and she seemed to get angrier. Plus, I saw Glynis go off for a smoke right before we found out she was dead. Glynis never smoked unless she was drinking." Holden shrugged again. "I think she found the wedding stressful. Glynis never did like being around crowds."

"So she drank to cope with the guests?"

"Yeah," said Holden. "I just wish she'd left the reception early if she'd been uncomfortable instead of drinking and acting out."

"Did you see anything? Anybody following Glynis? Or anything else that seemed to stand out?"

Holden said, "Not really. The only thing I thought was interesting was that two people who'd definitely not been invited to the wedding were there."

"Faith's father being one of them?"

Holden said, "Okay, then three uninvited guests. It seems like a lot of gatecrashers for a wedding. Besides Faith's father, there were Nash Moore and Belinda Clark. None of them were invited because Glynis couldn't stand them."

"Couldn't stand them? But I understand Glynis was dating Nash Moore." Myrtle thought it best if she acted as if she didn't know the story of Glynis's date life.

Holden snorted. "Yeah, but that didn't work out. I can't figure why Faith's aunt would have gone out with Nash, anyway. She likes to be the smartest person in the room and Nash would have given her some competition."

Myrtle said, "I understood from Nash that they had things in common."

"Did they? That's a surprise. Whenever I heard the two of them together, they seemed to be arguing over their differences. And when Nash showed up at the reception, I saw Glynis arguing with him. I noticed because I was worried Glynis was going to start ranting at him and make a big scene." He rolled his eyes. "Sure enough, she made a big scene later, except it was focused on me."

Myrtle said, "And then Belinda showed up?" She leaned in with an eager expression, as if she was just a harmless old lady looking for some gossip to liven up her day. Belinda had told her that she hadn't been at the wedding, so that was certainly news.

"No surprises there, really. Belinda followed Nash around everywhere. They'd been dating before Nash left her for Glynis. Unfortunately, I could tell Belinda was already tipsy. I figured it was better for me to get Belinda to leave than for Glynis to start yelling at her."

"Mercy. It all sounds very much like my soap opera, *Tomorrow's Promise*."

Holden looked as if he very much didn't want to talk about Myrtle's soap opera. He quickly continued, "Anyway, after I spoke to Belinda for a few minutes, she got all teary-eyed and agreed to leave. I was worried about her driving, but she said she'd call a friend and get a ride home." He shrugged. "So I guess she could have been there for a while, waiting for the friend to drive up."

"Long enough to take revenge on Glynis?"

Holden nodded. "I'd guess so. I mean, it wouldn't have taken long for someone to hit Glynis over the head."

"Poor Glynis," said Myrtle in a rather unconvincing voice.

Holden nodded again; his agreement also rather unconvincing. Then he stood. "Well, Miss Myrtle, I guess I'd better get along to my next job. You let me know if you have any more problems with mice, okay?"

"I'll be sure to. Thanks for coming by Holden."

After Holden left, Myrtle walked out to join Wanda on the dock. "He's gone," she said.

"Figured I'd let you visit. Find anything out?"

"Well, I found out that Belinda didn't leave the reception right away. And I found that there was an altercation between Nash and Glynis, although that's not much of a surprise." She frowned. "And while I was speaking with Holden, I noticed all the dust on my tables."

Wanda stood up. "I kin take care of that."

"Absolutely not. As I've mentioned before, you're my guest. I'll call that Puddin up right now. Last year I tried to get Puddin out near Christmas and neither she nor Dusty would ever pick up the phone."

"Got a plan to git 'em out here?"

"I certainly do. I'll continue phoning them until Puddin agrees to come over and clean. I'm up in the middle of the night, after all. I'll keep calling her at two-thirty a.m. and I bet she'll quickly capitulate. People like their sleep."

Wanda quirked a brow. "But not you."

"I like the small amount of sleep that I get. But I can't get hung up on how little I sleep, or I'd be frustrated every single night."

Wanda suddenly reached out a hand and a flash of black fur raced by and jumped on her lap.

"Pasha! Where did you come from?" asked Myrtle.

Wanda smiled. "Jest felt her presence behind us some-where."

The black cat nuzzled up against Wanda happily.

Myrtle said, "You two are so sweet together. And now I should call that Puddin."

As hard as it was to imagine, Puddin immediately picked up her phone. "Miz Myrtle," she said in a cranky voice.

"Hi Puddin. I need you to come over and give my house a pre-Christmas clean. The dust on my tables is really quite atrocious."

"Can't. Too busy," grouched Puddin.

Myrtle listened intently on her end of the phone. "It sounds like you're cleaning someone's house right now."

Then she heard a voice on the other end saying, "Puddin? Make sure you get the bathrooms this time."

Myrtle smiled. "That's Petunia Merriweather. She lives down the street from me. You can slide right by as soon as you're done there."

Puddin's voice was exasperated. "My back is thrown."

"If you can still clean for Petunia Merriweather, it's not thrown too badly. I'll see you in a few minutes." Myrtle hung up. "It's like herding cats trying to get Puddin to come out here."

Pasha jumped down from Wanda's lap to get some water and Wanda stretched. "Told you I could help you. Then you wouldn't have to git her over here."

Myrtle said, "No. You and I are going to watch some completely un-educational television."

And so Wanda and Myrtle were deeply entranced by a reality show about weddings. "This is making Faith and Holden's wedding not look that bad," muttered Myrtle.

Wanda said, "Nobody died at these weddin's on TV."

"But some of them should have. That one bride was really horrid."

The doorbell rang, and Myrtle gave a grim smile. "Finally."

Chapter Eleven

She opened the door and Puddin stood there with a sullen look on her pale face. "Here to clean," said Puddin unenthusiastically.

"Not without your cleaning supplies, you're not. You've nearly wiped out mine. Get your own out of the car."

Puddin slouched away and returned with an assortment of cleaning supplies in an old bucket. She walked in and gave Wanda a cautious nod of greeting. Wanda smiled at her.

Puddin set the bucket down on the floor with a clatter. This apparently startled Pasha, who flew out of the Christmas tree with a fierce cry.

Puddin shrieked and ran in the opposite direction.

Wanda tried to hide a grin.

"What was that witch cat doin' in the tree?" demanded Puddin.

Myrtle said, "Cats are quite fond of trees. I'm sure the little darling was simply trying to figure out what it was doing inside the house. She's quite intelligent, you know."

Puddin's beady eyes shifted suspiciously as they gazed around the room. "Where's she at?"

"After you terrified her, I'm certain she's gone off to recuperate. Really, Puddin, all that noise was completely unacceptable."

Puddin muttered something under her breath and proceeded to pull out her feather duster.

"Go shake that thing outside," said Myrtle. "In the state it's in, you're going to be depositing more dust than you're picking up."

Puddin stomped back outside.

Wanda suggested, "Mebbe we should git out of her way."

"Absolutely not. Puddin shouldn't interrupt anything we're doing. You and I are enjoying this wretched show and we should continue doing that."

The only problem was that Puddin, who was lackadaisically dusting the living room, was immediately, and predictably, drawn into the reality show.

"What's she doin'?" she asked breathlessly as one bride quit her job to plan her wedding full-time.

"Making a mistake," said Myrtle. "Which is precisely what you're doing right now, Puddin. You're intended to be cleaning."

"Am cleaning," said Puddin scornfully.

Myrtle deftly set the wedding show to record and turned off the television. "You were right, Wanda. It's better to watch the show later."

"Now I'm hooked," said Puddin. "You gotta let me see what happens next."

"If you finish my housekeeping, you can sit down and join us. Mercy. I can't even believe those words are coming from my mouth," said Myrtle with great annoyance at herself.

The upside was that Puddin finished her cleaning in record time. The downside was that it may have been completed in a rather slapdash fashion. Then the pale little woman plopped down on Myrtle's sofa and gestured at the TV.

"Well?" said Puddin.

Myrtle found the recorded show and the three of them watched the remainder of it. The bride who'd quit her job and her groom had gotten into a terrible argument (the bride wanted to spend too much money on the wedding and the groom was more financially conservative) and had broken off the engagement.

"Now she's broke *an'* single," noted Wanda thoughtfully.

"Serves her right," said the malevolent Puddin. "It was a dumb thing to do."

Pasha crept back up to Wanda and curled up in her lap again. Puddin eyed the feral cat with misgivings.

Myrtle rustled up some cash from her large handbag and handed it to Puddin. "I put a few extra dollars in there as a Christmas bonus."

Puddin's eyes lit up greedily, but then dimmed at the small amount.

"I'd give you more, but I just don't have it. This time of year, every penny is budgeted."

Puddin recognized the truth when she heard it. "Thanks," she muttered.

Wanda asked Puddin politely, "Whatcha doin' for Christmas?"

Puddin shrugged, "Same ole stuff. Dusty an' I get up and open presents. Then we eat a breakfast casserole, watch the parade, then take naps."

"What are you giving Dusty for Christmas?" asked Myrtle curiously.

"Fishin' stuff," said Puddin. "An' I know what he's supposed to be gettin' me." Her eyes narrowed at the thought of Dusty not purchasing his assigned gift.

Wanda looked worried, and Myrtle frowned.

"Is something wrong, Wanda?" asked Myrtle.

Wanda hastily shook her head.

Puddin said, "Well, I gotta get outta here. Lots to do." As an afterthought, she added, "Merry Christmas."

"Merry Christmas," said Myrtle as Puddin slouched back out the door.

"Now that the cleaning nonsense is over, let's make Christmas cookies," said Myrtle, clapping her hands together.

Wanda grew very still. "Okay. Want me to bake 'em?"

"I think we should make them together. That would be more fun, wouldn't it? I can do the mixing and you can do the decorating with the sprinkles and whatnot. Then we can bring them over to that cookie exchange."

Wanda quickly said, "I kin do the mixin'. You're better at the decoratin', I bet."

"My decorating skills aren't actually all that keen. I'll turn on some Christmas music so we can get into the cookie-making mood."

Myrtle did and soon the strains of music by Nat King Cole were wafting through the house.

"Let's see. First, we need to get a recipe. I have my mother's old cookbook for that."

The cookbook was indeed old. It was covered with the detritus of long-ago cooking, the binding had pretty much come apart, and the title of the book was completely indiscernible.

Myrtle carelessly flipped through the pages.

"Ain't you gonna break it?" Wanda winced at Myrtle's disregard for the yellowed pages.

"What? Oh, the cookbook? Well, it's mine to break. That's the attitude you have to have with old family things, otherwise you never use them. This cookbook is over a hundred years old, but if it's not used, it's no good to anyone. Do you have old cookbooks and mementoes?" Myrtle looked curiously at Wanda.

Wanda shook her head sadly. "Ain't really got nothin'. Family weren't like that."

Myrtle said, "That's a pity." She looked at Wanda and thought her friend looked sad, so she rapidly changed the subject. "Let's see. Maybe Mama's lemon cookie recipe would work."

Wanda blinked at the recipe that Myrtle gestured to. Her reading skills weren't particularly advanced. "What's that?" she asked, pointing to an unfamiliar word.

"Hmm? Oh, *oleo*. That's just an old word for margarine or oil."

Myrtle busily pulled out ingredients while Wanda squinted at the book and generally looked concerned.

"Not so many ingredients for this one," said Myrtle cheerfully.

"You got a lemon?" grated Wanda.

"Mercy! No, I haven't got a lemon. How silly of me."

Wanda quickly said, "Mebbe we should hold off on cookin.'"

"No sirree. Nothing is going to slow us down today. I'll call around and see if someone has a lemon. Miles might."

Miles, however, did not have a lemon. Furthermore, he sounded rather alarmed at the prospect of Myrtle baking cookies.

Myrtle hung up with a frown. "Miles isn't helpful."

"Mebbe Erma has a lemon."

Myrtle made a face. "Nothing is worth a visit with Erma."

She thought some more and then snapped her fingers. "Elaine. She's always cooking and baking and such. She might have a lemon."

Elaine did indeed have a lemon. Myrtle hurried across the street to collect it and to cuddle with Jack for a few minutes. She even sang him a rousing rendition of *Rudolph, the Red-Nosed Reindeer* while he grinned at her and touched her on the nose.

Wanda, back at Myrtle's house, painstakingly ran her finger across the recipe, word by word. As she did, she glanced around at the ingredients and the kitchen tools. Finally, she called Miles.

"Wanda?" asked Miles, sounding startled. "Is something wrong?"

"Myrtle's gonna crash the cookie party. An' I think the bakin' is wrong.

Miles said, "That sounds likely. Has she started yet?"

"Still collectin' ingredients. But I can't really read the recipe book."

Miles said, "How about if you take a picture of the recipe and send it to me? I'll read it out to you and you can take a look and see if she's on the right track." He paused. "Can your phone take pictures?"

Wanda's phone had been a very basic model indeed, provided by Sloan on behalf of the newspaper and in the interest of getting his precious horoscopes collected.

"Didn't used to, but Sloan upgraded me. Said it was fer Christmas. One second."

Wanda fumbled with the phone for a few minutes before taking a picture and sending it to Miles. The whole time, she kept a wary eye on the door in case Myrtle appeared.

On the other end of the phone, Miles studied the photo. Wanda also helpfully took a picture of the ingredients Myrtle had pulled out.

"She's got baking powder pulled out instead of baking soda," he noted. Then he added, "The recipe calls for sifting some of the ingredients, and I don't see a sifter." He sighed. "She doesn't always have the patience for baking. Myrtle usually just lumps things together and stirs them."

"Kin you read the recipe to me?" asked Wanda. She found a piece of paper and a stubby pencil.

Miles slowly read out the recipe while Wanda scribbled down a phonetic rendering of it that she would be able to read.

"Thanks," said Wanda. She hung up and quickly got to work. She burrowed through the cabinets until she found a sifter. Then she replaced the baking powder with baking soda. Myrtle had also taken out large measuring cups instead of smaller ones. Wanda managed to dig out some measuring spoons.

Wanda looked at the lemon cookies. "Don't think they need 'em."

"Cookies *always* need sprinkles."

"Think they might mess 'em up a little."

Myrtle looked thoughtfully at the cookies. "You think they're perfect as-is? That's nice to hear. All right, we'll leave them alone. I suppose I should let them cool off before I pack them up into containers."

The Christmas music was still playing in the background, and *I'll Be Home for Christmas* came on. Wanda had a dreamy look on her face. "Love this one," she said.

"Good memories?" asked Myrtle, hoping there were at least a few good ones from what often sounded like a rather hard life.

"My momma. She liked this one."

So they listened quietly for a while—Myrtle working on a crossword from her crossword puzzle book and Wanda playing solitaire.

Chapter Twelve

After a couple of pleasant hours went by, Myrtle said, "I suppose I should go to the grocery store. I'll need Miles to drive me."

"I could walk with you and hold half the bags," offered Wanda.

"Although that's most kind of you to offer, I think I might need substantially more than that. It's gotten close enough to Christmas that I feel I should do my yearly stocking-up. I get more than I usually buy in a week, so that I don't have to deal with crowds at the store. Or what qualifies as crowds in Bradley, anyway."

It sounded to Wanda like a big shopping trip, maybe even one long enough for her and Miles to slip away to the dollar store. "Elaine could take you."

"Oh, I don't think so. I've already troubled her for a lemon and three eggs, and that's likely enough for one day. Besides, she was about to put Jack down for a nap."

Myrtle called Miles. "Do you need anything at the store?"

Miles said slowly, "Are you offering to pick something up for me or asking if I can drive you and pick up something for myself?"

"Option two. I need a ride and I've pestered Elaine enough for one day."

Miles made a noise that sounded as if he'd been pestered quite a bit himself. Then he said, "I'll be right over."

And, in the vein of someone wanting to get something over with, Miles *was* right there. Myrtle barely had time to pick up her purse when she heard the light toot of his car horn indicating he was outside.

"Gracious," said Myrtle. "All right. Wanda, you help yourself to anything you want in the kitchen. Do you have any special requests for my grocery outing?"

Wanda looked suddenly serious. "Jest to be careful."

Myrtle frowned. "That sounds ominous. Is Miles going to have a car accident in the parking lot?"

Wanda shrugged a thin shoulder. "Jest got a bad feelin.'"

"Your bad feelings are worth taking note of. I'll watch my step," said Myrtle grimly. Then she hurried off to Miles's car.

When she climbed in, she carefully put on her seatbelt. Then she peered across to ensure Miles was wearing his own.

"Something wrong?" asked Miles.

"Wanda has a bad feeling about our outing."

Now Miles looked a bit panicky. "Maybe we shouldn't go. I have food at home. I can bring over sandwiches and we can go to the store tomorrow instead."

"That sounds rather silly. She didn't tell me not to go, only to be careful. Which we should fully intend on doing."

Miles set out for the short trip to the Piggly-Wiggly grocery store, driving about twenty miles an hour and looking around him as if expecting meteors to fall from the sky onto his sedan.

"I don't think we have to fear for our *lives*, Miles. That didn't seem to be the impression I got from Wanda."

"I don't know, Myrtle. Isn't this about the time when a second murder happens?" asked Miles glumly.

"What an odd thing to say!"

"It's an accurate thing to say. I just want to make sure the second murder isn't one of us. Or *both* of us." Miles knit his brows and continued driving with fierce concentration.

A few moments later, Myrtle said, "Stop the car."

Miles came to a skidding stop. "What is it? What happened?"

"I didn't mean for you to stop the car in the middle of the street, Miles! Here, turn off down that side street. I just saw something we should investigate."

Miles looked mulish. "I don't think it's a good idea. Remember what Wanda said."

"We'll carefully watch our steps as we investigate why Belinda Clark is walking with great determination up to Nash Moore's house."

Miles's expression turned to a squeamish one. "We shouldn't insert ourselves in the middle of that. It's some sort of mess with their love triangle."

"If a third of the love triangle is deceased, I don't believe it's a triangle anymore. Perhaps it's a line. A love line."

Miles had no interest in discussing romantic geometry with Myrtle. "I still think it's a bad idea."

"Then I shall investigate by myself." Myrtle opened the car door.

"Close the door; I'll drive over."

Myrtle looked smug as she closed the door and they headed over to park in front of Nash's house.

It was quite a substantial, dignified-looking brick house on a quiet, tree-lined road off the main street.

"Won't he think it's odd that we're here?" asked Miles unhappily.

"Of course not. I'll just say we wanted to check in and see how he was doing. He'll simply think I'm a nosy old woman."

"Imagine that," muttered Miles.

They trudged up the front walk. Despite Myrtle's cane pounding on the cement, Belinda was so entirely focused on summoning Nash to the door that she didn't notice they were there. There was also a man next door who was staring at the commotion from his front porch, who went entirely unnoticed. Finally, Miles gave a dry cough to indicate their presence.

Belinda jumped, then looked relieved as she saw who was there. Then she looked a mite embarrassed. "Hi."

Myrtle said, "Hi, Belinda. Miles and I were just driving by on our way to the store and saw you here."

Belinda gave her a weak smile.

Myrtle said, "You know dear, you were right when you said it was better that you'd had a glimpse of Nash's proclivities before you ended up engaged or married to him. He appears to have the morals of an alley cat. I think it's best that you don't pursue this any longer. Miles, who is proficient in the ways of men, also agrees."

Miles appeared startled by his agreement.

Belinda hung her head. "I know you're right. But maybe something happened to Nash. He's obviously here—his car is right there in the driveway. I called the hospital, and he's not scheduled to work. He's not answering the door, though. I've rung the bell *and* knocked."

Myrtle said, "Yes, but he might just not *want* to answer the door. That's always a possibility."

Belinda shook her head stubbornly. "He might avoid my calls and texts, but he wouldn't avoid me in person."

"Let's see if he avoids *me* in person," said Myrtle. She rang the doorbell numerous times in a row and called out in a peremptory manner, "Nash! Answer the door so we can clear up this matter of whether you're all right or not."

There was no response.

Miles said slowly, "It is rather hard for someone to ignore consistently ringing doorbells." He gave Myrtle a meaningful expression that harkened back to their earlier conversation about second bodies. "Perhaps we should call the police."

Belinda turned pink. "The police will think I'm wasting their time, won't they? Won't they be working on the case?"

Myrtle said, "Then we'll go inside ourselves. Have you checked the door to see if it's locked?"

Belinda shook her head.

"Miles, perhaps you should go inside first in case Nash is in a state of *dishabille*," said Myrtle.

Belinda's eyes grew wide. "You think he might be sick?"

"No, I wonder if he might be fresh out of a shower. Partially clothed. It might be best if Miles went in first."

"Maybe he *was* in the shower," said Belinda. "He works such odd hours that he takes showers at unusual times."

Miles, not particularly happy with his assigned task, squared his shoulders and tried the door. It opened as he turned it. "Hello?" he called into the house.

There was no answer from inside, so Miles cautiously ventured further. "Nash? It's Miles Bradford here with Myrtle Clover and Belinda." He couldn't seem to summon up Belinda's last name.

Hearing no answer, the three made their way further inside the house, with Miles at the lead. "Nash?" he called anxiously.

When they moved from the foyer to the living room, Miles stopped. "Oh, no."

Nash was in front of his massive fireplace, dead.

Chapter Thirteen

B elinda gave a shriek and rushed forward before Myrtle stopped her by grabbing her arm. "It's a crime scene, dear."

Miles gingerly stepped forward to put a finger where Nash's pulse should be. After a few moments, he shook his head.

Belinda sobbed. "Nash."

Myrtle frowned, staring at the scene. "The weapon is that piece of wood."

"A yule log," said Belinda through her sobs. "Nash had a yule log. He said it was a family tradition."

Miles said, "Myrtle, we should call Red."

Myrtle gave a blustery sigh. "I suppose."

"And go outside," said Miles in a rather insistent voice. He was never fond of proximity to bodies and seemed to find himself in situations where they were frequently littered around.

She pulled her phone from her tremendous purse and slowly followed Miles and Belinda outside.

Red answered immediately. "Mama? You all right? You didn't take a fall or anything?"

"I certainly haven't done any such thing. I'm just being a good citizen and calling to report an issue."

Red sighed. "What did Erma do now?"

"As a matter-of-fact, I'm certain Erma's light displays violate town ordinances. There are far too many lights, they're far too bright, and they're on far too late at night. You should know all of this, considering the fact you're directly across the street from her."

Red's voice was grating on the other end. "Mama, I'm busy."

"I'm busy too. I've just discovered Nash Moore's body."

"*What*?"

"That's right," said Myrtle with a sniff. "Nash is at home. I suggest you come here post-haste." She hung up.

Belinda was something of a mess. She was shivering and crying and looking as if she might fall over at any moment.

"Perhaps we should move Belinda to my car," said Miles with concern.

"Where's Belinda's car?" asked Myrtle.

Belinda wiped away some of the tears so she could see Myrtle. "I walked over. I thought if Nash saw my car, he wouldn't open the door. But he wasn't going to open the door, anyway."

A fresh bout of tears began, and Myrtle hastily located some tissues from her purse and thrust them at Belinda. She needed to ask Belinda a few questions while she was off-balance and before Red got there and ruined everything.

"Belinda, you'll be all right. Let's have a seat here on the front steps."

Belinda kept sobbing.

Myrtle said sternly, "Settle down, now. You're upsetting Miles."

Miles, who'd been absently listening to the far-off squeal of a siren, blinked in surprise at his name being mentioned.

Belinda, not wanting to be the reason to upset an elderly man, quickly pulled herself together.

"Now, Red is probably going to ask you some questions, considering the circumstances," said Myrtle in a calm voice. "Perhaps it would be a good idea to run through exactly what you're planning on telling him before he arrives."

She cut right to the chase because the siren was getting closer, although it was still fairly far away.

Belinda's teary eyes were open wide. "You think he's going to think I had something to do with Nash's death? But I loved him!"

"Love and hate can be very similar feelings, dear. Can you tell him where you were up until you were at Nash's house?" asked Myrtle. As Belinda seemed slow to take in her meaning, she asked, "Do you have an alibi?"

Belinda rubbed her eyes. "Not really. When do I need one?"

Myrtle looked at Miles, who had at least checked Nash for a pulse. Miles cleared his throat. "Perhaps for last night?"

Belinda gave a short laugh. "I was with my daughter, of course. Not that she's much of an alibi since she was asleep by eight p.m."

"Nevertheless, you were at home all night?" asked Myrtle.

"Of course. I would never endanger my daughter by leaving her in the house by herself. She's in school right now or else she'd be here with me now. I tried to sleep last night, but I tossed and turned in my bed. I ended up reading in the hopes of getting sleepy, but it didn't work."

"What were you reading?" asked Miles with interest.

Myrtle gave him a look through narrowed eyes. There was no time for the niceties as the siren grew ever closer.

Belinda paused and then said, "Oh, I'm horrible remembering titles and author names. Um, let me see. It's a book I enjoyed as a child—*A Wrinkle in Time*."

"Madeleine L'Engle," said Miles with an approving nod.

Myrtle cut in quickly, "I suppose re-reading books one read as a child is very soothing. And you've had a tough time recently, haven't you?"

Belinda nodded, looking weary. "That's right. The whole night I realized I needed to hear from Nash's lips that we were truly over."

"But I thought the whole point was that the relationship *had* been over," said Myrtle. "It sounded as if Nash had made that very clear." It was difficult to keep the exasperation out of her voice.

"But things might have changed with Glynis gone," explained Belinda. "I couldn't take the chance on losing out on a relationship with him. He could have felt completely differently now."

Myrtle found that highly unlikely. And Miles looked as if he'd rather be anywhere else than involved in a conversation that clearly didn't make sense to him.

"By the way," said Myrtle, "has Red asked you why you were there at the wedding? Perhaps you'd better prepare a ready answer for that."

Belinda shrugged. "It's pretty straightforward. I was just trying to find an opportunity to speak with Nash and try to reason with him. I'd heard Glynis had dumped him and I wanted to see if we could get back together and continue our relationship. I didn't care a whit about harming Glynis. Besides, I wasn't the only one at the wedding who wasn't invited. Nash wasn't supposed to be there, either."

Nash, of course, was now dead. It now didn't seem at all likely that he'd murdered Glynis.

Belinda continued, "I just don't know what I'll do without Nash. I'm so baffled that he didn't understand how precious our relationship was. The fact that he threw it all away to be with someone like Glynis completely stumps me. Did you see how she acted at the reception? Yelling at her son-in-law? I can't imagine Nash wanting to be with her."

"There are plenty more fish in the sea," said Myrtle. She was hearing the police siren coming down the street. But then she heard a train whistle and smiled. That would hold Red up for a few minutes, at least. "He wasn't that great of a catch, anyway."

Miles agreed. "If his affections shifted that rapidly, he doesn't sound as if he was a good prospect."

"Have you thought more about who could be responsible for these crimes?" asked Myrtle.

Belinda nodded. "It took me a while to realize it, but when I was at the reception and trying to find a good time to catch Nash alone, I noticed Faith's father following Glynis around."

Myrtle raised her eyebrows. "I'm surprised you even realized who he was. He left Bradley quite a long time ago."

"I *didn't* know who he was, actually, you're right. But I overheard two older ladies talking about him and looking his way. I think he's called Edgar? Anyway, he looked as if he'd had a lot to drink. I saw him slumped over the table and staggering around, too."

Myrtle nodded her head, trying to get the last bit of information out of her before the train finished crossing and Red was there on top of them. "Were Glynis and her brother arguing?"

"Not that I saw, but she was furious with him for being there. I heard her talking about it. If *Edgar* had ended up dead, I'd have known right away who did it."

There was a slamming of a car door, and they turned to see Red approaching them. A moment later, another car pulled in.

"Detective Perkins!" purred Myrtle as the two men hurried up together.

Red sighed and turned to Miles. "Inside the house?"

"Near the fireplace," said Miles helpfully.

Perkins murmured, "It's good to see you, as always, Mrs. Clover. I'll be right back."

The two men weren't right back, actually. They were inside for several minutes, surveying the scene. When they exited the house, they looked rather grim.

Perkins gave them all a solemn look and pulled out a notebook. "Who was first to arrive?" he asked.

Belinda looked a bit uncomfortable. "I was. But I had no idea what had happened inside. I was trying to speak with Nash."

"About?" Red quirked an eyebrow. Myrtle had the feeling Red knew exactly why Belinda had been at Nash's residence.

"I was just trying to speak with him. About . . . well, about a private matter."

Red said, "Unfortunately, Belinda, there really aren't any private matters during a police investigation."

Belinda looked over to Perkins for confirmation, and he nodded.

She took in a deep breath and said, "All right. I was there, trying to see if Nash and I could patch up our relationship and try again. I was sure we were meant to be together."

"So you thought with Glynis out of the way, you'd have a shot at dating him again," said Red. He narrowed his eyes.

Belinda stumbled over her words. "No. That is . . . I guess that's right, but you're making it sound wrong. Glynis had broken up with Nash. The only problem was that he was focused on trying to get her to get together with him again."

Myrtle and Miles looked at each other. Belinda didn't seem to realize she was doing the same thing . . . trying to force someone to continue a relationship.

Perkins said softly, "So you came over here to speak with him at home. And he didn't answer the door. What did you think happened?"

"Well, at first I thought he was just ignoring me like he'd ignored my calls and texts. Then I starting really banging on the door and ringing the doorbell. That's when Miss Myrtle and Mr. Bradford came up."

Myrtle preened. Miles gave a tight smile.

"What amazing timing," muttered Red.

Myrtle said, "We could see Belinda was quite distressed. We decided to come over and see if we could help."

"You weren't following Belinda around?" asked Red suspiciously.

"What—stalking her? What fabricated nonsense, Red. Of *course* we weren't. Miles and I were on our way to the grocery store and just happened to be driving past at that particular moment. Anyway, we found it rather odd that Nash wasn't answering his door, despite the persistent racket Belinda was making."

Miles cleared his throat. "It was the type of clamor that would have been difficult to ignore."

"Miles very cautiously stepped inside first and then we followed. That's when we saw poor Nash in front of the fireplace."

Belinda gave a sob and Red looked warily at her as if she were a bomb about to explode.

Perhaps Perkins thought the same, because he tweaked the subject a bit. "Had Nash been seeing anyone else after Glynis broke up with him?"

Belinda's expression was scornful. "Only that Blanche."

Red's eyebrows flew up. He turned to his mother. "Your Blanche?"

"Well, she certainly isn't *my* Blanche, but she's the one in my garden and book clubs. There are no other Blanches in town."

Red must have seen an idea forming in Myrtle's mind. He said sternly, "Under no circumstances are you to head over there. I'll send my deputy her way in a few minutes." He glanced over at the state policeman beside him. "You have any other questions you'd like to ask, Perkins?"

The officer shook his head. "Thanks for filling us in, Mrs. Clover."

Myrtle smiled at him, and Red rolled his eyes.

Belinda, looking rather relieved, quickly said goodbye and walked away.

After she was out of earshot, Myrtle said, "Lieutenant Perkins, I did have one question for *you*. You're always so very helpful. I was wondering if there had been much forensic evidence near Glynis. Footprints and whatnot. I thought it would be lovely if there were really good prints."

Perkins gave her a polite smile. "I wish there had been, Mrs. Clover. Unfortunately, with the lack of rain, there weren't any helpful footprints. There are a few items that our forensics team is taking a closer look at. I wouldn't be able to disclose anything of that nature, unfortunately."

"Witness statements? Anything helpful from the other guests at the wedding?" Myrtle asked sweetly.

Red muttered, "It's an interrogation."

Perkins said, "We didn't really acquire any useful information, I'm afraid. It seemed most of the guests had been drinking and weren't completely clear on the order of events."

Myrtle nodded. "There was quite a bit of drinking going on that night. That's not surprising at all."

Red said in a tight voice, "If that's all, you're welcome to move along, Mama."

Myrtle shot him a look, but she and Miles headed toward his car. When they got inside, Myrtle said, "Mercy! What a day."

Miles said, "I'm actually feeling slightly better."

"Better? After finding Nash on the floor of his living room?"

Miles considered this. "Perhaps it's because the second victim has now been identified. And it's not either of us."

"Very true." Myrtle paused. "And Wanda did warn me about going out today. We got through it unscathed, though. And now everything seems different, doesn't it? Nash likely didn't kill Glynis at all. If he did, that means there are two murderers."

"Which has happened before."

"Yes, but I don't really get that multiple-murderer feeling here. Let's operate on the belief that Nash didn't harm Glynis. That means it must be Faith, Holden, Edgar, or Belinda. Or Blanche, although she seems rather unlikely, doesn't she?"

Miles said, "Or someone we haven't found a motive for yet."

"I don't think so. In this town, we'd have already heard about anyone with a grievance against Glynis. You know how Bradley is."

Miles did indeed. "What if Nash's murder is unrelated? Perhaps he royally messed up someone's surgery."

"Then killing him with a yule log would be a silly way of rectifying that. That's what medical malpractice lawsuits are for. No, we have to go with the supposition that Nash's murder was related to Glynis's." Myrtle glanced through the window. "Why aren't we moving? Aren't you going to start driving the car? We're still in Nash's massive driveway."

"I was waiting for directions," said Miles.

"You know perfectly well how to get to the Piggly-Wiggly."

"I meant I wanted to make sure that going to the grocery store was still our plan. Our errand was completely hijacked. I thought perhaps you'd want to head home and figure out our next steps," said Miles.

"Certainly not. Now we have more reason than ever to go to the store."

Miles was a bit concerned about what she meant by that statement, but obediently drove the short distance to the store as Myrtle looked thoughtfully out the window.

When they walked inside, Myrtle said, "Now I need to figure out what to cook for Blanche."

Miles's eyes opened wide. "Blanche?"

"Of course. She's just lost her boyfriend."

"Blanche may not even *know* she's lost her boyfriend," said Miles. "Plus, we were expressly told by Red not to go over there."

"Red said he was sending a deputy there to break the news to her. Besides, Red *always* tells me what to do and not do, and I rarely listen to him. Let's see. Blanche likes to eat, so it should be easy to figure out what we should bring to her."

Miles quickly said, "You know what Blanche *really* likes to do? Drink. Perhaps we should simply bring her a good bottle of wine."

Myrtle frowned at him. "You bring wine to people who have something to celebrate. This isn't exactly cause for celebration, although I do think Blanche had a lucky escape in some ways. Once a cheater, always a cheater."

"She could drown her sorrows with the wine."

"Miles! You sound positively desperate. I appreciate your fervor, but we should think of something more practical for Blanche. A casserole, for instance."

"How about something sweet? Like these cupcakes?" Miles helpfully pointed out a nearby display.

"Santa cupcakes with sprinkles? Really, Miles. It simply wouldn't be appropriate."

Miles looked wildly around him. "There are charcuterie trays over there. That would be easy. We could just run it by."

"What a peculiar suggestion! Blanche isn't giving a party; she's grieving a lost love. Besides, I'm somewhat low on funds right now with the upcoming holiday and having shelled out for a wedding gift for Faith and Holden. Charcuteries are rather pricey."

Miles said, "We could just visit with Blanche, offer our condolences, and then leave without bringing anything at all. Blanche and Nash weren't married, after all. They were simply dating each other and not for very long, at that."

Myrtle looked horrified at the notion of not bringing food. "I just don't think I have it in me, Miles. Going empty-handed into a situation like this just doesn't seem right. My mother would be rolling in her grave."

"Then bring Blanche a flower arrangement instead. I know—you could bring her one of the poinsettias you took from Tippy's house."

"I didn't *take* them, Miles. They were party favors. And Blanche would have gotten one, as well."

Miles said, "I doubt she did. She was too intoxicated to remember to take party favors home with her."

"You're so insistent! All right, then. The poinsettia it is. Now let's get our grocery shopping done so we can make the trip to see Blanche."

The shopping took very little time because Myrtle's list was carefully organized by aisles. Miles had a few impulse buys, including, rather inexplicably, a can of organic, unsalted black beans.

They put their groceries away at their individual houses, Myrtle grabbed the poinsettia, and then they set off to see Blanche.

Miles, driving, said, "Wanda didn't want to come?"

"She very politely declined. But then, Blanche always pesters her for fortunes whenever Wanda is around. That would get very tiring, you know."

"What kinds of fortunes does Wanda generally give Blanche?" asked Miles curiously.

"You know, the typical. She'll meet someone new and they'll start a relationship." Myrtle shrugged. "They always come true, but then Blanche would make them happen, wouldn't she?"

Chapter Fourteen

Blanche's house was a nice brick home, surrounded by lush landscaping. The deputy had already left, fortunately, and Red and company didn't appear to be on site yet. "Perfect timing," said Myrtle.

Blanche answered the door immediately. She was wearing all black and some very grim makeup that appeared to be hastily applied. "How sweet of you both," she murmured, looking at the plant. "Won't you come in?"

"We were so sorry to hear about Nash," said Myrtle, as sincerely as she could say it. "It must be such a terrible shock for you."

Blanche nodded sadly. "I couldn't believe it, Myrtle. Simply *couldn't* believe it. I made the deputy say the words three times before they even started sinking in. Why, I only saw Nash yesterday and he was fit as a fiddle."

Myrtle resisted the strong urge to remind Blanche that it wasn't illness that felled Nash.

Blanche continued, "I couldn't face the day after I heard the news. My world had grown dark and cold, so I put on black to match it." She blinked mournfully at Miles, who gave her a startled smile.

"And I see you closed all the blinds," said Myrtle. "To further reflect your mood."

"Hmm? Oh, no, that's just because I'm hungover. Blasted vodka."

A chuckle started bubbling out of Miles, which he hastily converted into an awkward-sounding cough.

Blanche said, "You're both so kind to understand what I'm going through. I know it wasn't as if Nash and I were married, or even engaged, but it's still a loss, just the same. Another prospect bites the dust." Her eyes glowed with sudden malevolence. "Somebody's gotta be punished for that."

"Any ideas who?" asked Myrtle.

"Absolutely. I think it's that nutty Belinda. She's been giving me the stink-eye every time I see her out and about. What a ridiculous woman."

Miles said mildly, "I thought she was rather nice. Although perhaps misguided in terms of relationships."

"You're only thinking she's nice because *you're* nice, Miles," said Blanche. "I tell you, the woman is off her rocker. I guess Belinda took offence that I started dating Nash because she's been calling me at all hours of the day and night and then hanging up."

"But you know it's her," said Myrtle.

"The silly woman is one of the contacts on my phone! Of course it's her. I finally blocked her number and haven't heard from her since then. What's annoying is that the deputy was asking questions as if *I* had something to do with Nash's death." Blanche gave an inelegant snort.

"Were you able to provide the deputy with an alibi?" asked Myrtle.

"Sure was. I was out partying with Georgia last night. We tied one on at the bar downtown. Your boss at the newspaper saw us there, too. What's his name?"

"Sloan," said Myrtle. She found it very plausible that Sloan had been frequenting the bar.

"Right, Sloan. Anyway, Georgia knows how to live it up. We were doing vodka shots for a while and I couldn't keep up with her."

Miles looked intrigued.

"I danced with Sloan and Georgia danced with lots of people. The bar finally kicked us out to close up, and she and I staggered back to our respective homes since nobody could drive."

"And Nash wasn't with you?" asked Miles.

"Nope. He said he had to work." Blanche shrugged.

"Really? He didn't seem to be attired for working," said Myrtle.

Blanche's eyes grew big. "Oh my gosh! You were the ones who found him?"

"I'm afraid so," said Myrtle, as if discovering bodies wasn't something of a regular occurrence.

Blanche frowned. "I can't remember if Nash had to work during the time Georgia and I were heading downtown or if he had a late shift and needed to sleep before he went to the hospital. Either way, it was work that stopped him from going with us."

"Of course I don't want to upset you any more than you already are. But I was wondering if you could talk about your general impressions of Nash."

Blanche considered this, picking at the sleeve on her black top. "Well, he was smart."

Myrtle nodded. That went without saying, considering his profession.

Blanche seemed to be searching for other traits of Nash's. She smiled as she finally hit on one. "He enjoyed reading. Nash talked about joining our book club."

"That would have made Miles happy," said Myrtle. "Imagine another man at book club!"

Miles looked wistful.

Blanche was now really reaching. "Um. Well, he had a nice house." She paused. "We didn't really go out for very long, Myrtle. We were just starting to get to know each other when tragedy struck."

Myrtle and Miles shared a quick glance. It was clear that pumping Blanche for further information would be futile.

Myrtle gave Blanche a smile. "Thank you. And now Miles and I really should be going. I know you'll likely want some time alone to reflect."

Blanche looked a bit startled, as if that wasn't what she planned on doing whatsoever. "Right. Thanks to the two of you for coming by. And for the poinsettia."

Myrtle pursed her lips. "I thought I should bring over some home cooking, but Miles disagreed."

Blanche gave Miles an intensely grateful look. "A plant is perfect."

Myrtle and Miles took their leave and drove away.

"Where to?" asked Miles, very much hoping the answer was *home*. He didn't particularly care which home it was, only that it was one of theirs.

Myrtle said, "Let's go to the diner. They'll still be barely serving breakfast now and I have the hankering for their lumberjack breakfast."

"The diner? But we've just been to the grocery store. We could eat cereal or something."

Myrtle said, "Yes, but the thought of making food right now is not a bit appealing. I have a bit of money in my discretionary fund, and I believe a few dollars of it can go toward eating out. But we should swing by and pick up Wanda. She'll want to eat out, for sure."

When they arrived at Myrtle's house, Wanda was sitting quietly on the front porch. She rose and walked over to the car when she spotted them.

"Knew we were coming, did you?" asked Myrtle. "It's very handy having a psychic as a friend."

Miles gave a shiver, as he often did when Wanda did something he couldn't scientifically explain.

Wanda drawled, "Goin' to the diner? I got a little money to spend there."

"My treat," said Miles in a rote manner.

"For me, too?" asked Myrtle, delighted.

Miles gave a small sigh and nodded.

Bo's Diner had been a fixture in downtown Bradley since Myrtle was a child. There had been generations of owners, but the restaurant never really seemed to change. Now it was decorated for Christmas with lights strung outside and red and green spotlights shining on the building.

The spotlights made Myrtle think of Erma's lights. "Wanda, are Erma's lights driving you crazy? They're dancing around my room all night. Visions of sugar plums are dancing in my head in a most nightmarish way."

Wanda said, "Nope. Sleepin' like the dead."

Miles shivered again at the mention of the dead.

Myrtle frowned at him. "Are you all right, Miles? You seem to be shivering quite a bit. You don't have any sort of fever, do you? Octogenarians are quite susceptible to fevers."

Miles gave her a wry look. "Are they? You're rarely under the weather."

"At any rate, keep your germs to yourself if you're feeling poorly. Sharing isn't caring in this particular instance, especially with Christmas fast approaching."

They walked inside to more Christmas decorations involving large amounts of colored tinsel on the vinyl booths. A waitress quickly seated them.

Myrtle said, "We haven't even had the chance to tell you about our morning, Wanda."

Wanda gave them a sad look. "Tole you not to go."

"Did you know about Nash?" asked Miles, frowning.

Wanda shook her head. "Jest knew somebody was dead. An' you was headin' toward 'em." She picked up the menu, which fortunately had helpful pictures to assist with any unfamiliar words.

Myrtle said, "The lumberjack breakfast is good. That's what I'll likely get. They do offer fairly boring breakfast options here, too. Miles ordinarily goes for oatmeal for some unknown reason."

"It's very good," protested Miles.

"It's the same exact oatmeal you could prepare for yourself at home," chided Myrtle. "At least get cheese grits. You are in the South, after all."

The waitress appeared, called them all "hon" and took their orders. Miles reluctantly got the cheese grits. "You'll love 'em," promised the waitress as she walked away.

Myrtle peered at the door. "Holden Davis is coming in."

"The poor man is probably trying to grab something to eat before he hurries off to the next pest control appointment. We should leave him alone," said Miles.

Myrtle appeared not to have heard this objection. "Holden? Over here."

Miles gave a gusty sigh as Holden spotted Myrtle and came over.

"Won't you join us?" asked Myrtle, reverting to her tremulous needy old lady persona. "We'd so like the company, wouldn't we, Miles?"

Miles gave Myrtle an annoyed look.

"And Wanda, I'm not sure if you've met Holden."

Wanda gave Holden a polite gap-toothed grin.

Holden hesitated for a split second before graciously saying, "That's awfully sweet of you, Miss Myrtle. As long as it's okay that I have to leave soon to get to my next appointment."

"Of course. I was a working woman for many years after my husband died. I know exactly what you're talking about."

Miles slid over in the booth and Holden sat down next to him. The waitress came over, smiled at Holden, and took his order.

Then Holden said curiously to Myrtle, "What was it that you used to do when you were employed?"

"Well, as you might guess, there weren't so many options for women in those days. I didn't fancy myself as a nurse."

Miles's expression suggested that he was trying and failing to picture Myrtle as being deferential to a doctor in any way.

"So I went into teaching. Actually, I think I was best suited to teaching. Although, if I'd been born in a different generation, I believe I could have been an astronaut. I've always had a great interest in science."

"Wouldn't *that* have been something?" asked Holden admiringly.

Miles's expression now suggested that the idea of Myrtle terrorizing the universe was hilarious.

Holden asked, "Any more problems from our furry friend?"

"My mouse? He's not taken the bait yet. I suppose he's very canny, having had to live by his wits his whole life," said Myrtle.

"You have a mouse in your house?" Miles frowned.

"It's only a tiny thing, Miles. You don't have to be worried about it."

Miles said, "It's not the size that worries me. It's the fact it could be creating all sorts of unsanitary conditions in your house. Besides, I thought your cat would take care of extermination. That's sort of the species' stock in trade."

"Pasha was the cause of the mouse being there to begin with. The little love was bringing me a gift. She's very clever. And determined. The poor dear thinks I'm completely hopeless at hunting. Pasha has tried to educate me in the ways and means of hunting before, but it didn't take. I suppose she's trying to take one more stab at it. She must wonder how I'd do in the wild."

"Poorly," decided Miles.

"Well, if I were *hunting*, I'd say I wouldn't do well. But I have the feeling I'd be a very adept scavenger. After all, I know exactly the right places to go."

"Which are?" Miles lifted his eyebrows.

"Tippy's trashcans, for one. She always has this really elaborate food, over plans, and then ends up tossing the bulk of it. I'd eat like a queen out of her rolling bin."

Holden asked, "What kinds of things has Pasha been bringing over?"

"Gracious, it's been all sorts of little creatures. A couple of shrews, a chipmunk, a squirrel, and a rabbit. All of them were live and got away outside because Pasha left them on my doorstep. But *this* time she decided an indoor lesson might work better. She's very ingenious, you know. Because of the number and frequency of these gifts, I'm convinced she's reenacting *The Twelve Days of Christmas*. The only problem is that she doesn't seem to realize the twelve days of Christmas technically *starts* with Christmas. It's supposed to be the span of time between the birth of Christ and the appearance of the Magi. The Epiphany."

Holden was looking drowsy, whether from lack of sleep, the company, or the conversation. He blinked a few times and straightened up in his seat to shake it off.

"But now you've distracted me, Miles, with talk of theology," said Myrtle crossly. "I can't even remember what we were talking about before you started ruminating on religion."

Miles sighed.

"I believe we were talking about the mouse," prompted Holden. "What I think you might want to try is a change of bait."

The waitress came over with Myrtle and Miles's order. "Here you are, loves. Do you need anything else, my dears?"

Myrtle said, "Maybe some ketchup. I think our container is a bit low."

The waitress smoothly switched out their ketchup containers, smiled at Holden again, and hurried away.

Holden continued, "Instead of the cheese, you might want to try peanut butter. Mice really enjoy seeds and nuts. Chocolate is a hit with them, too."

Miles looked unhappy at further conversation about mice while he was trying to consume his breakfast.

"Thanks, Holden. I'll certainly give that a try. I'm glad to see you today and not just because of my mouse issue. What do you think about Nash Moore's death?"

Miles sighed again as the conversation continued veering into areas that weren't suitable for consuming food. Wanda held back a smile.

Holden's eyes grew. "What? Nash Moore is dead?"

Chapter Fifteen

People at several tables turned to look at them now. The news would definitely be making the rounds.

"I guess the news hasn't quite made it around town yet, which is certainly surprising. Perhaps it's because everyone has Christmas on the brain. Yes, Miles and I were with Belinda Clark this morning when Nash was found. It was all most disturbing." Myrtle took an unconcerned bite of her lumberjack breakfast.

"I was with Lucinda Barrett all morning," said Holden slowly. "I guess that's why I haven't heard."

Myrtle scoffed. "Lucinda Barrett could have someone directly telling her about Nash to her face and she wouldn't hear it. She's deaf as a post." She paused. "I suppose Red will be paying you another visit."

Holden paled. "Will he?"

"He typically follows up with everyone he spoke with the first time. It's procedure, of course. But perhaps you have an alibi?"

Holden looked vastly relieved. "Yes. Lucinda Barrett, as I just mentioned."

"I believe the alibi probably needs to be for *last night*. From what we could tell, anyway. Miles was the one who actually handled the body, of course."

Miles was looking at his food with complete disinterest now.

Holden said, "I was home with Faith, of course. I guess we'll just be the alibis for each other. Surely Red doesn't think we had anything to do with Nash's death. You mean it was a murder? Somebody killed Nash Moore?"

The various ears at the other tables pricked up again, and it became silent in the busy diner.

"Terrible, isn't it?" asked Myrtle.

Holden nodded wordlessly.

"Did you know him?" asked Myrtle, with her most innocent of expressions. "I suppose you must have spent time with him, considering he was seeing Glynis."

"Not really," said Holden slowly. "I mean, I met him a couple of times when I was picking up Faith from Glynis's house when we were dating."

Wanda looked thoughtful at this assertion.

"What did you think of him?" asked Miles, pushing his meal aside.

Holden shrugged. "He was pretty intense. Real smart, but that's not a surprise. He was a surgeon and everything."

Myrtle noticed Holden wasn't looking them in the eye anymore. She frowned.

Just then, the waitress came back with Holden's plate. He seemed grateful for the distraction.

"Anyway," he said, "I'm hoping Red is going to wrap this case up pretty fast. It's been real hard on Faith. It's kind of a rough way to start out a marriage." Holden finally looked Myrtle in the eye again. "I was wondering if you were on the case. Maybe you can pick up on things that Red can't."

Myrtle was pleased as punch to hear this. "Why, yes. Yes, I am on the case."

Holden relaxed a little. "Faith told me you were an investigative reporter for the paper. I hope you figure it all out soon. I'll give you as much information as I can to help you out. Like I said, Faith has been a real wreck lately. She feels guilty about Glynis because the last few weeks were rough with the wedding planning and all. I think I mentioned that to you last time."

"Weddings are always stressful," said Myrtle in the tone of someone who has been to scads of them over the course of eighty-plus years.

"Yeah, that's what everyone has been telling Faith. But she feels bad because she felt like things weren't real good between Glynis and her. The guilt is eating her up. I was just thinking, if somebody could figure out who did this, Faith can divert all those feelings to the killer."

Myrtle said, "Well, never you fear. I am on the case." She paused. "Perhaps it would be better if you didn't let Red know that, though. He tries to stymie everything I set out to do."

"My lips are sealed." Holden made a zipping motion over his mouth.

"Good. Now, who do you think might be involved in these crimes? You're out and about in the community a good bit as an exterminator. Have you picked up on anything that might prove helpful?"

Holden ate for a minute, thinking it over. "I know he's Faith's dad, but it sure seems to make the most sense that he's the one who's responsible for all this."

"How so?"

"Well, Miss Myrtle, I'll level with you. I think he's bad news. I tried to be decent about Edgar at first because he's Faith's father and everything. But to be honest, the guy is just slimy. I can see how stressed-out Faith is around him, so I don't want him anywhere near her. He wasn't around when she was little and needed him. Now she *doesn't* need him, she's come into some money, and he won't leave her alone." Holden made a disgusted sound.

Myrtle finished her breakfast, which she had dispatched in record time. "Has the will been executed yet? That is to say, did Glynis leave her brother anything from her estate?"

Holden snorted. "Not a dime. That's no surprise because Glynis couldn't stand the guy. From what I've seen, she used really good judgment staying away from him. Glynis left her money to Faith and a bunch to charity."

"That must be nice for a young couple just starting out in the world," said Myrtle.

"It is. I mean, we were never really worried about money, anyway. I've never minded doing an honest day's work and Faith's the same way. But now we have a nest egg, if we need it."

Myrtle asked, "Did Glynis's house go to Faith, too?"

"It did. She's going to try to sell it. The place is just way too big for us and full of memories for Faith. We'd rather start a completely new chapter." Holden pushed the food around on his plate. "The way Edgar has been hanging around really disgusts me. He's acting like he expects Faith to let him live at the house, rent-free, for the rest of his life."

Miles said, "You say he's been hanging around a lot. Is he spending a lot of time with Faith?"

Holden nodded. "Pestering the life out of her, more like. He acts like the last couple of decades never happened. But he didn't earn the right to be part of Faith's life."

"You're absolutely right," said Myrtle. "He seems like a really dreadful man. I remember his father was the same exact way. Shifty."

"Yeah. I mean, we've got enough going on right now without having to handle him, too. Glynis's funeral is tomorrow. I'm hoping the service will provide closure for Faith." He glanced at his watch and shoveled food into his mouth.

"Well, we hope the same thing."

Holden swallowed down the food and sighed. "I guess she won't *really* have closure until after the perp is caught, though."

"That's likely the case. I know you're about to have to head off to your next client's house, but I wanted to tell you that you conducted yourself beautifully at the wedding reception. I don't think I mentioned it to you before. But when Glynis was acting so disgracefully, you really kept your cool."

Holden smiled at her. "Thanks. It took a little effort. I mean, I have a pretty laid-back personality, but I did see red when Glynis went off like that. I was mad at Glynis because she made Faith so upset when Faith had put so much time and thought into making our wedding meaningful. Once I saw Faith's face, though, I managed to calm myself down. I didn't want to make a bad situation worse." He glanced at his watch again. "And now, I'm sorry, but I do have to run. Good seeing y'all and meeting you, Wanda. And Miss Myrtle, let me know if I can give you any kind of info to help you wrap this case up."

With that, Holden grabbed the check and hurried up to the register to pay the bill.

Wanda croaked, "Nice boy."

Myrtle frowned. "So Holden isn't a suspect?"

"I can't tell who is and who ain't."

Myrtle said, "We should move on to something more tangible, then. Like dessert."

Miles looked scandalized. "Dessert? But we just ate breakfast."

"Who says we can't have dessert after breakfast? I still have a bit of room in my tummy for something else. How about you, Wanda?"

Wanda nodded.

"The best part is that Bo's Diner has a special Christmas dessert menu." Myrtle brandished the laminated paper that had been tucked away behind the napkin holder. "They have plum pudding, apricot and walnut fruitcake, candied pecans, and gingerbread."

"Mmm," said Wanda, looking as if she hadn't yet eaten a bite of food instead of having polished off an entire plate.

Miles still looked confused about eating dessert. "Are we going to get the dessert to-go so that we can enjoy it later? After we're hungry again?"

"Wanda and I are both hungry now. You haven't even finished your cheese grits, so you *should* be hungry."

"It was the discussion of mice and murder. It made my stomach turn on me."

Myrtle said, "I think you need to show your stomach who's boss. Anyway, why not try some of the dessert? You can always take it home with you if you can't eat it now."

Which was how they ended up with candied pecans and gingerbread at the table. The gingerbread was so good that Miles relinquished the cheese grits entirely and had the dessert be his breakfast.

Once Miles had taken the last bite of his gingerbread, Myrtle said, "Okay. So let's talk about murder now that Miles has finally finished eating. Wanda, what are your thoughts on the Nash and Glynis deaths?"

Wanda finished chewing a candied pecan and said, "It don't look good for nobody."

"Not even Faith? Or her charming new husband?"

Wanda shook her head. "Nope. 'Cause they git money."

"Very true. Although it certainly doesn't sound as if money is a major driver for them. Holden has talked extensively about job satisfaction and putting in an honest day's work. It doesn't seem as if it's very important to them."

Miles said, "It might be one of those things where they realize they *do* like having money after they get it."

"Yes. Money would be a major motive, of course. But they're very sweet young people. I hope they're not responsible for all this."

Miles offered, "It might not be a money motive for Faith and Holden. It could be that they lashed out at Glynis because of the way she made a big scene at the reception. One of them could've had an angry moment with her and murdered her in a blind rage."

"Again, true. Okay, so we've established there are plenty of motives between them. Who else do we have?"

Wanda croaked, "Edgar?"

"Well, nobody seems to like him," said Myrtle. "He wasn't invited to the wedding and yet he was there. Money would obviously be his motive—he doesn't have any and he needs some. He clearly hasn't treasured his family connections, so I don't think he'd have a tough time murdering for financial gain. He's definitely a contender."

Miles said, "And then there's Belinda. I thought she was acting completely irrationally today."

"Indeed she was. The very idea of trying to get back together with someone who'd already left you for someone else! She didn't seem to be able to be dissuaded that she was looking at it the wrong way, either. Not until we found Nash."

They were quiet for a moment, reliving the morning. Then Wanda said, "Might've been angry with Nash. Gone after him for leavin' her."

"Love and hate are very similar emotions, aren't they?" mused Myrtle. "Well, I guess we'll just have to ruminate on it some more. We can mull it over until we get the answer. And now I suppose we should go pay and head out on our way. I have a cookie swap to attend."

Miles and Wanda exchanged a look.

Miles said, "How did you even find out the precise information for the event? Considering the fact you weren't invited."

Myrtle said smugly, "When I was chatting with Puddin, she gave me all the details. Her cousin cleans for Tippy."

Miles and Wanda exchanged looks again. It had been very sly of Puddin to provide the information. But then, Puddin always appreciated a bit of chaos.

"Have you tried the cookies? The ones you're bringing to the swap?" asked Miles.

"Of course not! The cookies aren't for me . . . they're for the swap. That's the way it works. And you should come with me, both of you. You're both very popular."

Wanda and Miles quickly shook their heads. Miles said, "After this heavy breakfast, I'm ready for a long winter's nap. Besides, *one* person gatecrashing a Christmas cookie swap is one thing. *Three* people seems more like a coup."

"I suppose you're right, although I do think the two of you are being fuddy-duddies."

Miles paid for their meals and then took them home. Myrtle wrote up her article on Nash's demise for the paper while Wanda curled up on the sofa and drifted off to sleep.

Myrtle walked into the back of the house so she wouldn't wake Wanda by talking on the phone. "Sloan? I've got another article for you. You'll want to make sure it runs on the front page tomorrow."

"Is it the piece on Christmas memories?" asked Sloan hopefully.

"What? Oh. No, that's not it. And frankly, Sloan, that piece was fine before Bradley became murder central, but I don't seem to have the time for it now."

"Murder central?" Sloan sounded rather bemused.

"Nash Moore is dead."

Sloan groaned on the other end. "So another crime story."

"Only because there's another *crime*. Anyway, I know you have that intern. I have the feeling she'd really enjoy writing a story about Christmas memories."

Sloan's voice was uncomfortable. "Well, I'm not sure her mom and dad would want me sending her around to knock on doors with a killer at large. It might be dangerous."

"That's the best part of my idea. You should have her *email* people or contact them on their social media. You know how good kids are on social media. She could even pull quotes from the stories and put them up on the internet. It will be perfect."

Sloan sounded less-convinced but also as if he didn't really want to argue. "Okay, Miss Myrtle."

"I'm sending over the feature on Nash Moore. Toodle-oo."

"Toodle-oo," said Sloan miserably.

With that out of the way, Myrtle could watch her soap opera, which she'd taped earlier. Wanda managed to rouse herself awake for the show and they watched as more Christmas-related drama ensued. One character who was on life support suddenly started speaking, rose from her bed, and was soon waltzing under the mistletoe with her beau.

"Seems kinda impossible," noted Wanda.

"Doesn't it? I suppose the writers wanted to include a feel-good Christmas miracle in the script. Or, perhaps, there was some *deus ex machina* at work," mulled Myrtle.

Wanda said, "Reckon that's Latin."

"An excellent call. Yes, it is."

Wanda said, "Whut does it mean?"

"Basically, that the writers have employed a plot device. It's a bad thing."

Wanda yawned, looking drowsy again. "Mebbc so. But it was still a good show."

"Yes, it was." Myrtle squinted at the clock. "Mercy! It's time for me to go to the blasted cookie swap."

"Thought you *wanted* to go."

Myrtle said, "I certainly do not. I've hung out with those ladies enough lately. But I do so dislike not being invited to things. It irks me. That's why I'll be there."

"An' Tippy won't mind?"

Myrtle said, "I'm sure Tippy *will* mind. She'll mind that I've found her out. But Tippy would never say so. They'll all act as if I was invited all along. Besides, octogenarians can crash as many parties as we like and no one would ever say a word." She frowned. "The only thing is that I hate the idea of you being here by yourself so much. Are you absolutely sure you won't go with me?"

Wanda shook her head. "Actually, Miles and me is goin' out."

Myrtle's eyes opened wide. "Really? That's very nice. What . . . a sort of cousins outing?"

"Mmm," said Wanda in a noncommittal way.

"Well, I hope it's fun. Now I feel better about leaving you behind." She picked up the carefully-wrapped plate of lemon cookies and said, "See you in a bit."

There were quite a few cars at Tippy's house. Apparently, everyone in Bradley had been busily baking. Myrtle basked in the surprised looks she received when she walked in the door.

Chapter Sixteen

E rma Sherman gasped, "She wasn't on the guest list!" Tippy shot Erma an annoyed look and swept over to Myrtle's side. "Myrtle. What a pleasure to see you."

"And it's such a pleasure to be here. I don't know where this town would be without you, Tippy. I do believe you're hosting at least half of the events in town this Christmas."

Tippy gave her a gracious smile. "It's something I enjoy."

Everyone seemed to watch Myrtle's plate of cookies with great intensity.

Tippy said, "How about if you put your treats over here in the display area?"

Myrtle followed her into the dining room and watched as she put the lemon cookies down on a massive mahogany table that easily seated twelve. Everyone else watched, too.

"You should try one," said Myrtle. "It's an ancient recipe from my mother's cookbook."

Tippy froze. Then she slowly said, "As tempted as I am, I believe I'm right at the limit of my daily caloric intake."

"Nonsense! I know how organized you are, Tippy. If you knew you were hosting a Christmas cookie swap, and I presume you did, you'd ensure all of your calories were consumed during your party."

Tippy gave her a small smile. "Of course." She reached out for a lemon cookie.

Everyone was completely silent, watching the tableau unfold.

Tippy broke off a bit of the cookie and put it in her mouth. Her eyebrows went up, and she thoughtfully chewed it. Finally, she swallowed it down and said, "Delicious."

The proclamation appeared to stun the audience. There were murmurs of surprise.

Myrtle preened.

Tippy considered Myrtle for a few moments. "You must have worked very hard on these."

Myrtle snorted. "It was child's play. It *is* an excellent recipe, however. You're all free to ask me for it. Wanda gave me a hand in the kitchen—she was my sous chef."

There were quick glances among the revelers.

Tippy gave her a smile. "I can imagine that Wanda was a tremendous help."

"Well, I didn't really *need* tremendous help, since this was a fairly easy recipe. But yes, she was very helpful, as always."

Tippy nodded. "Be sure to sample everyone's goodies. We'll do a recipe swap later."

The conversations started up again, and soon the house was buzzing with it. Tippy moved on to greet some new arrivals while Myrtle picked up a plate of fine china and handpicked seven cookies to place on it.

She turned around to find Erma Sherman standing impossibly close to her with a leering grin on her face.

"So Wanda helped you out with your cookies, did she?"

Myrtle said coolly, "Wanda is a friend of mine. I like to include her in as many activities as I can while she's staying with me."

"Did her crazy brother run her off?" asked Erma with interest.

"Certainly not. She's merely made the sensible decision to spend Christmas with friends."

"But she's not here," said Erma, looking around.

"No. More's the pity. I wanted her to come with me, of course. She had a conflict, however. Plus, she'll likely want to take a nap. Considering how it's been so very bright outside with your Christmas lights."

Erma, not particularly sensitive to subtext, said, "You're investigating these murders, aren't you? There's something you probably should know. Something *important*."

Erma always liked to think everything she observed was especially significant. Unfortunately, it rarely was.

Myrtle was deliberately about to forego whatever silly thing Erma thought was notable information and bring up the Christmas lights again when Erma continued.

"I've been having these really rotten GI issues," said Erma.

Myrtle closed her eyes. "Not the time nor the place, Erma."

Erma blithely persisted, "You wouldn't believe how terrible they've become. Anyway, I had a colonoscopy scheduled."

Myrtle began looking desperately around for an escape route.

"So I was driving early that morning. Although I think *next* time, I'll have the colonoscopy in the late afternoon because I was up all night drinking that horrid preparation."

"There's someone I should talk to," said Myrtle in a tight voice. Then she frowned. "Wait a minute. You couldn't have been driving *yourself* to your colonoscopy. It's simply not allowed."

Erma gave her donkey-like grin. "You're right. Sandra Sotheby drove me. Anyway, that's not pertinent. Do you want to know the point of the whole story?"

"Yes, I do," said Myrtle fervently.

"Well, it was early in the day, like I said. The sun hadn't tossed its rays onto the earth. The world was still under the cover of darkness."

Myrtle frowned at Erma. She was getting entirely too florid with this story. But then Erma rarely got her attention to this degree and was trying to make the most of it.

Erma finally got to the promised point of the story. "We drove by Nash Moore's house and guess who was there?"

"Nash?"

"Besides Nash. *Belinda*. She was there!"

Myrtle considered this. It was very possible that Erma's definition of "very early in the morning" differed greatly from hers. Maybe Erma had passed by just a minute before Myrtle and Miles had. "Did you see Belinda knocking on Nash's front door and calling for him?"

"No, no. I saw her acting *sneaky*. She was looking like she was doing something underhanded. Can you believe it?"

What Myrtle couldn't believe was that Erma had kept this story to herself. Not only had she just told Myrtle the story, it was probably the umpteenth time she'd told anybody. And it likely had additional embellishments each time it was told.

Erma must have noticed the doubtful expression on Myrtle's face. "It's the absolute truth."

"It sounds very odd. I saw Belinda later, and she was knocking on the door."

Erma shrugged. "Maybe she left and came back and tried to get him to answer the door."

"Or maybe you saw her when I did, or just moments before." Myrtle paused and then grimly continued, unable to help herself. "On a completely different matter, I wanted to broach the subject of your Christmas lights."

Erma lit up. "Aren't they super? I spent a lot of time stringing those up. I meant to put them up earlier in the season, but I've been busy with health issues."

Myrtle crossed her fingers that Erma wouldn't feel obliged to go into the health issues. For once, Erma didn't delve into the foul details, but continued, "Have you noticed the tinsel trees in the yard? The lights bounce right off them and you can really see the colors of the trees. You know, pink, silver, and gold."

"Yes, but it's the *lights* that are the problem, you see. It doesn't matter where they reflect from."

Before Myrtle could give a soliloquy on the importance of using timers for Christmas lights, Tippy was asking for everyone's attention. Erma spotted someone else across the room who she wanted to bother and scampered away. Myrtle sighed that she hadn't been able to put her point across, but felt tremendously relieved at the same time that Erma had left her presence.

Tippy thanked everyone for being there and then announced the winners of the best cookies from the votes she'd collected from the judges.

Myrtle's lemon cookies won third place.

Everyone gave a very loud round of applause as Myrtle curtsied. "It's my mother's recipe," she said with a shrug.

Annie, one of the judges, said, "It's just so different from everything else. Unique."

"Old," said Myrtle. "Well over a hundred years. I suppose it's not popular anymore and the lack of popularity makes it rare and interesting."

She received a white ribbon for her third-place win and placed it carefully in her large purse. Myrtle smiled smugly.

She was so pleased with her win that she later put the ribbon up in her kitchen. And somehow, even with the crazy Christmas lights streaming on her walls, she fell into a very satisfying sleep.

Chapter Seventeen

The next morning, Myrtle got ready for Glynis's funeral. She got dressed early this time because there always seemed to be mishaps regarding her funeral wardrobe.

She'd anticipated that with all the festive Christmas activities, her funeral clothes might be a little tight on her. She'd even gone to the trouble of purchasing special undergarments intended to compel oneself into an outfit. To her delight, however, she somehow appeared to have lost a small amount of weight and could easily slip into the clothes.

Miles arrived promptly thirty minutes before the service to pick up Myrtle. Wanda declined when Myrtle asked her if she wanted to go. "Cemeteries is loud places for me," she said with a shrug.

Myrtle thought that sounded like a reasonable excuse for a psychic to make. Miles shivered.

The service was graveside and, according to the local gossip, had been in accordance with Glynis's own, very detailed instructions. Faith and the minister were merely there to ensure everything went according to plan.

One thing that had perhaps *not* gone according to plan was the appearance of Edgar Ross at the funeral. Although Glynis was Edgar's sister, Myrtle had the feeling Glynis wouldn't have welcomed his presence there. He was wearing the same suit he'd worn to his daughter's wedding.

Miles quietly observed Edgar, who seemed to have found some friend from the old days there and was laughing with him. Miles murmured, "He appears rather peppy for being at his sister's funeral."

"Well, they weren't all that close, after all. But his behavior does seem to be upsetting Faith."

Sure enough, Faith was watching her father with a worried look on her face.

Miles said, "Just the same, it seems a bit disrespectful to be laughing right before a funeral starts."

Tippy quickly joined them, looking a bit harried, which was unusual for Tippy.

"Everything all right?" murmured Myrtle.

Tippy nodded, smoothing down her immaculate black dress. "It's fine. I simply got busy with work-related things and time got away from me. Thank goodness the service hasn't started yet."

"Did you know Glynis well?" asked Myrtle.

Tippy gave a slight shake of her head. "Not really. I think Glynis liked keeping to herself most of the time."

Miles said, "I suppose she must have been involved with the church. Considering the service, I mean."

The graveside service did indeed seem to be geared toward churchgoers. Aside from the minister, there were a couple of folks in choir robes who seemed ready to burst into song at any time.

Tippy said, "She was a very important member, although a quiet one. Glynis didn't serve on any committees or volunteer, but she was always there and seemed to get something out of the services. She also was very generous with her donations."

Myrtle figured as much. "Such a terrible chore for Faith. It's too bad that she had to plan her aunt's funeral. Unless what people are saying is correct and Glynis had the whole service laid out."

Tippy said, "The gossips are right, at least in this instance. Glynis was so very organized, you know. She planned her own service from beginning to end. Faith only had to print out the instructions for the minister."

Miles said slowly, "But she had no inkling she was going to pass away, I'm assuming. Unless you're saying that there was some sort of overt threat Glynis was responding to when she penned her instructions."

"Nothing like that, no. But Glynis had an entire file she'd labeled 'in case of my demise.'" Tippy seemed to realize she appeared to know a lot about the situation. "I went over to give Faith a hand at Glynis's house. But once we found that file, everything was easy. Glynis had even written her own obituary."

"Gracious," said Myrtle.

The service started then. Glynis had chosen some rather somber hymns for her service, "Abide with Me" being one of them. The small choir did an excellent job, however, and it was all very moving. The pastor stumbled through a couple of rather bleak Bible passages Glynis had specified. There seemed to be a general air of relief when the service drew to an end. They all adjourned to the church hall for the reception.

The church hall was decorated for Christmas and seemed very jaunty for a funeral reception. The church ladies made sure the atmosphere was somber, however—they frowned as they served food for everyone. And food there definitely was. There were, in fact, so many different types of casseroles that everyone felt quite overwhelmed when trying to choose amongst them.

After they'd gotten their plates filled with food, Miles murmured, "Do you have a plan as to where you'd like to sit?"

"Well, I'd like to speak with Edgar Ross. But it appears he's lighting from one table to another, like a social butterfly. I guess it doesn't really matter where we sit."

They found a quiet little table for just the two of them. That way, if Edgar happened by, they'd be able to talk with him in private.

Miles had tried to stick with eating fruits and vegetables. Fruits and vegetables at a Southern funeral, however, were not necessarily straight-forward. He had green bean casserole that was loaded with mayonnaise, fried okra, and a sugary pineapple casserole.

Myrtle said, "Mercy, Miles. I think you might have a heart attack from trying to be healthy. There's a heap of cholesterol on that plate."

Miles looked morosely down at the food. "It's as if they're deliberately trying to sabotage my good intentions." He glanced over at Myrtle's plate. "What's all that?"

"Who knows? It was all buried under cream of chicken soup. One thing I know, though—it will be good. These ladies know how to cook." Myrtle peered across the room. "It looks like Edgar might be wending his way to us."

Edgar was. He plopped down to join them. "How are you two doing?"

Myrtle said, "Oh, we're fine. We wanted to tell you again how sorry we were for your loss."

Edgar shrugged it off. "It's all right. I mean, it's all very sad, but we all have to die sometime, don't we? And this is a nice send-off for Glynis. I think she would have liked it."

Miles said, "We understand Glynis planned the funeral herself."

Edgar snorted. "That's right. Sounds like Glynis, doesn't it? At least Faith didn't have to do a bunch of planning. I have the feeling that Nash didn't do the same thing. Who knows who'll be making plans for his?"

Myrtle hadn't thought of this. "That's true. He doesn't seem to have any family in town."

"Did you know him?" asked Edgar curiously. "I just know what Faith has told me about him. I don't think Faith was all that crazy about him."

"Wasn't she?" asked Myrtle innocently.

"That's right. She thought he was sort of stuck-up. You know how surgeons can be. They think they're the best."

Myrtle said, "Well, they sort of *are* the best. When you need surgery, anyway. I can see where they'd develop those sorts of complexes. And, no, to answer your question, Miles and I didn't really know him at all. We saw him just recently at a book club Christmas party. I think he enjoyed doing things out and about."

"Which I can understand," said Edgar with a grin. "I like going out, myself. If I have an opportunity to be social, I'm there. It's one reason I attended my dear daughter's wedding."

Myrtle thought that Edgar also seemed to view the funeral as a chance to be social, judging from what she'd seen.

"I wanted to mention something, since I know this town likes to talk. I wanted to explain why I was out the night Nash died. Somebody spotted me walking around and I don't want anyone to get the wrong idea. You see, I'm something of a night owl. I'm sure the two of you turn in real early so you probably won't understand that." He gave a chuckle.

Myrtle raised her eyebrows. "On the contrary, Miles and I are both insomniacs. We stay up late and get up early. We fully understand."

Edgar looked slightly taken aback. "Okay, got it. Anyway, I'd gone out for a stroll right before I turned in. Sometimes it's good to stretch my legs for a few minutes before I sleep."

"Did you sleep well?"

"Like a log," said Edgar. "I'm the kind of person who can sleep through anything, though. A nuclear bomb could go off and I'd be snoring right through it."

Myrtle pressed her lips together in annoyance. She felt people really shouldn't brag about sleeping well. It was most obnoxious.

Edgar said, "Your son did come around to talk to me about Nash." He put a hand playfully to his heart. "It wounded me. I can't see how anybody would think I had something to do with killing my sister or this surgeon."

Miles asked, "You didn't know Nash?"

"Now, how could I? You know I don't live here and haven't for gobs of years. My sister had broken up with Nash by the time I came into town. I saw him at the reception, but I knew Glynis sure hadn't invited him from the way she was staring daggers at him. All I really knew is what I've heard about him through Faith. Which isn't much."

Myrtle said, "Well, I know Faith because she's my beautician. She wrestles my hair into shape beautifully. I do think Faith is a very sensible young woman. Did she shed any light on Nash and what he was like? Or why Nash and your sister broke up?"

Edgar snorted. "Oh, I know why they broke up. It was a battle of egos."

"What's that?"

"Egos. Glynis had a huge ego. She'd always thought a lot of herself. In her case, though, it was probably warranted. She was a smart cookie. Plus, every surgeon I've ever had the misfortune of meeting has had an equally big ego. I bet that bothered Glynis. She liked being the smartest person in the room."

Myrtle said, "That makes sense." She paused. "I've been wondering if you've made any more plans. I know you were talking about settling here in Bradley, in Glynis's former home, I believe."

A dreamy look came into Edgar's eyes as he contemplated it all. "That's right. I have ideas about making that house look the way it *should* look. Glynis was all into minimalist design, which I've never been crazy about. Plus, the walls and stuff are just white everywhere. I never understood the love for neutral colors. That place needs some livening up!"

Myrtle said, "For some reason, the talk around town is that Faith intends to sell the house. That it's too large for Holden and herself."

A rather petulant look came across Edgar's features. He said, "You know how people like talking in Bradley. But I think you'll find Faith wants me to live in the house. I'm her dad and I really don't have anyplace else to go. Faith will grow to like the house a lot more once we completely redo it. I'm envisioning different colored paint in every room, but having it *coordinate*, you know? We definitely need to sell Glynis's furniture and get some more contemporary things. Glynis's style was sort of stuffy. Anyway, I'm here to stay. I know I wasn't always the best dad for Faith and wasn't always around. But life is for making amends, isn't it?"

With his rather impassioned speech, the scent of alcohol wafted through to Myrtle's nostrils. She wrinkled her nose.

Edgar looked at Miles. "You're kind of a quiet type, aren't you? I bet you spend a lot of time thinking."

Miles looked rather startled to be called out. "Me?"

"That's right. You're one of those who likes to sit around taking it all in and then coming up with ideas."

Miles seemed taken aback by this assessment.

Edgar said, "So tell me—who do *you* think murdered Glynis and Nash? Got any inklings?"

"I really don't know," said Miles. There was a hint of coolness in his voice that Myrtle knew meant that he wanted Edgar to back off.

Edgar said, "Don't want to share, huh? Well, I've been thinking, too. I think my dear son-in-law might have had something to do with it."

"What makes you think that?" asked Myrtle.

"Plenty of stuff. I mean, Holden and I probably got off on the wrong foot to start out with, but I think Holden isn't exactly what he seems like. Right?"

"How so?" asked Myrtle.

"He has this act, like he's this mild-mannered exterminator. But the truth is more complicated than that. I don't think he's as harmless as he looks. I saw Holden's face when Glynis was insulting him at his own wedding reception. Believe me, I recognize hate when I see it."

Myrtle asked, "You think Holden hated Glynis?"

"I think he did right in that second, sure. You know how people can get when they're really angry—he might have seen red and then took her out. Plus, he and Faith could have used the money at the time, too. My daughter would have nothing to do with it, of course. I don't know Faith as well as I should, but I know she's always been a straight arrow."

Miles said slowly, "Did you see Holden at all when your sister stepped away?"

"I knew Faith was asking people to find Holden because it was time to cut the cake. There were so many guests that they'd gotten separated from each other. At their own wedding! Anyway, she didn't ask me, but I decided to look around a little."

"Faith was surprised you were there, I'm guessing," said Myrtle.

Edgar shrugged. "Surprised, but happy. Glad to see me."

Myrtle was impressed by Edgar's ability to deceive himself.

"So when I looked around the crowd for Holden, I didn't see him. I figured maybe he was in the men's room. So I trotted up to Glynis's house to see if he was in there. But he wasn't there." Edgar shrugged again. "Where was he? Maybe he'd followed Glynis to give her a piece of his mind. He's got his pride, right?"

"No one seems to have seen Holden slipping away," noted Myrtle.

"It was pretty chaotic there. Lots of drinking and dancing and eating. Folks are *supposed* to be there for the bride and groom, but it's really an excuse for a party. The bridesmaids and groomsmen were toasted. I don't think anybody was tracking Holden's movements whatsoever. And the photographer was one of those who tries to capture the artsy side of the wedding with the setting sun and the trees—that kind of nonsense. He wasn't keeping track of where Holden was, either." Edgar said, "On a side note, I always told Glynis her smoking habit was eventually going to kill her. And it did!"

Not exactly in the way he'd thought it would, however. Myrtle pressed her lips together.

Edgar looked around the reception. "Sorry to cut this short, but I gotta go speak to more folks. Good seeing the two of you. Thanks for coming out."

And with that, he rushed off.

Miles looked after him. "It's almost as if he's acting as a host at the funeral."

"That's how he likes to think of himself . . . a master of ceremonies."

Miles asked, "Do you think he's really that outgoing? Or is there an underlying reason he's working the room?"

"He's totally networking. Edgar should be finding himself a job. Not only that, he should be finding himself a place to *rent*. No matter what he thinks, those two kids are going to sell Glynis's house and find something more suitable for them. Edgar is probably also trying to ensure his reputation is intact and that no one thinks he murdered Glynis or Nash."

They finished eating and spoke with Faith and Holden for a few minutes before heading out.

Miles said, "I hope you're planning on going home for a little while."

Myrtle raised her eyebrows. "You hope? You're not wanting to visit with Wanda and me?"

"It's not that I don't want to. It's that I really, really need a nap. I think it's all those heavy vegetables hitting my stomach. I feel very lethargic."

"Hearing you talk about 'heavy vegetables' is funny, Miles."

Miles protested, "They *were* heavy. They were all embedded in casseroles or smothered in gravy. They were decidedly not a vegetarian's vegetables."

"Then it's a good thing you're not a vegetarian. But we digress. Of course, you can take me back home. I ate a lot of food, too, and I think I may take a walk to help me digest it. Perhaps Wanda would like to stroll with me."

So Miles dropped Myrtle off at her house and proceeded home with some relief for a long winter's nap.

Chapter Eighteen

Wanda was waiting for Myrtle. She had her new, second-hand tennis shoes on and had a gap-toothed grin on her face.

"We gonna walk?" she asked.

Myrtle said, "As I've said before, having a psychic around is most convenient. A walk sounds fantastic and will prevent me from falling into a food coma. Let me change from my funeral clothes."

A few minutes later, garbed in slacks and a cotton blouse, Myrtle joined up with Wanda, and they set out on their walk.

"Where to?" asked Wanda.

"Well, usually I go in the opposite direction of Erma's house. I'm always terrified she's going to see me walking from her window and sprint out to join me. So let's head this way."

They set out through the neighborhood. Wanda was the perfect person to walk with. She didn't run her mouth a lot, and she was very interested in all the little observations Myrtle had about the houses and neighbors along the way, which pleased Myrtle.

One house they passed belonged to Georgia Simpson. On the outside, Georgia's house appeared perfectly normal. On the inside, Georgia had decorated it very eclectically. She was a huge fan of browsing garage sales and flea markets and her house clearly reflected that hobby. Myrtle particularly remembered Georgia had once picked up a casket that had been built but then had somehow gone unused and had turned it into a coffee table. She also had a collection of angels that she was very proud of.

Today, Georgia wasn't at a flea market or garage sale, but in her yard. Georgia made quite a picture with her big hair that was sprayed into submission and her tattoos covering her arms and legs as she battled some apparently tenacious weeds in one of her beds.

She spotted Wanda and Myrtle and raised a hand in greeting. As she walked over, Myrtle saw Georgia's tee shirt sported a rather rude saying. Myrtle graciously ignored it.

"Well, hi there, girls," said Georgia in her booming voice. "Getting a little exercise?"

Myrtle said, "We're just stretching our legs a bit. I think *you're* getting more exercise."

Georgia shot an exasperated look at the garden bed. "I'll say. I don't know what those weeds are, but they're really brawling with me." She grinned at Wanda, "Hey, I didn't know you lived around here. That's really cool. Maybe we'll all see you out and about more."

Wanda drawled, "Ain't livin' here . . . jest visitin' Myrtle a while."

"I thought it might be more fun to have Wanda stay with me for Christmas since her brother is out of town," said Myrtle. "Do you have plans for Christmas?"

"Do I? I sure do. I'm going gambling at that casino in Cherokee. It's going to be a blast." Georgia's mascara-encrusted eyes opened wide as she had a thought. "Hey, want to come along? It would be something totally different for you."

Myrtle hastily said, "Thanks, but I'll be spending time with Red and family."

Georgia nodded. "Of course you are. I didn't think about it. I don't have any family I keep in touch with, so it never comes to mind. What about you, Wanda?" Her eyes gleamed. "I think you and I could make for quite a winning team at the casino."

"I think yer winnin' plenty as it is."

Georgia guffawed. "You're right about that. It depends on what games I play, of course. I make sure I don't play the ones that I have the worst luck at. Unlike some people."

Wanda looked over at Myrtle as if she knew who Georgia might be referring to. But Myrtle didn't, so she asked, "Was there somebody we know who likes to gamble?"

Georgia nodded, her stiff hair not moving a centimeter. "Holden used to be a regular over there. I mean, I don't go but about once a month. But every single time I'd go to the casino, I'd see him there. That tells me he was there an awful lot. And he really could have used Wanda's help. There's one important thing about gambling; you can't gamble more than you're prepared to lose."

"And he was?" asked Myrtle.

"Oh yeah. He was the kind of gambler who kept going when he was losing because he figured his luck had to turn at some point. He'd keep going because he needed to make up his losses."

"So you think he was in debt?" asked Myrtle.

"Unless he's made of money. Which I doubt he is."

Myrtle said, "That's really sad. I wonder if Faith knew that before they got married. Young people shouldn't have to start out their lives under the burden of debt like that."

Georgia shrugged. "I don't know. I haven't seen him out there *recently*, so maybe he's resolved to keep away from the casino."

A trickle of perspiration ran down Georgia's brow and she impatiently rubbed it away, causing her mascara to smear across her face in the process. The mark gave her a somewhat sinister appearance, despite her grinning face.

"Well, it was good talking to you, Georgia. We'll let you get back to your weeding."

Georgia said, "Come back anytime. Next time, I'll invite you inside!"

As they walked away, Myrtle said, "Let's walk back to the house. There are a few things I need to catch up on there." She paused. "And I want to think about what Georgia just told us."

"You think Holden had somethin' to do with all this?" asked Wanda.

"I hope not," said Myrtle. "He seems like a very nice young man. It doesn't sound good, though, does it?"

When they returned to the house, Myrtle turned on some classic Christmas music as she tidied up the kitchen. She turned to see Wanda looking at the tree wistfully. Upon closer study, Myrtle thought Wanda appeared rather sad. Myrtle quickly changed the playlist to pop-oriented songs that were a lot peppier. She didn't like seeing anyone sad, but especially not Wanda.

There was a knock at the door and Wanda opened it since she was closer.

Elaine smiled at Wanda. "Hello there! Merry Christmas."

"Merry Christmas to you," said Wanda.

Jack bounced in, looking curiously up at Wanda before giving Myrtle a hug around the leg.

"I had a big favor to ask you," Elaine said to Myrtle. "And don't worry—it's not the Christmas play again. You got those kids into shape. But I need to do some last-minute Christmas shopping. Do you think you could watch Jack for a little while?"

"Oh, it would be my pleasure. We'll have a good time, won't we, Jack?"

The little boy was hopping from one leg to the other. "Kissmas comin'!" he proclaimed.

"It certainly is! Would you like to play with Miss Wanda and me for a little while?"

Jack gave a solemn nod as his mother gave him a quick hug and slipped away. Then he ran over to the closet to pull out the basket of toys that Myrtle kept just for him.

Myrtle and Jack played with trucks and blocks for a while. Wanda unobtrusively did some cleaning up, knowing Myrtle would stop her if she noticed. The Christmas music played peppily in the background.

Myrtle's only requirement for the truck-and-block game that she and Jack had made up was that it had to be played on the table so that she didn't have to get on the floor. It wasn't that Myrtle particularly had anything against playing on the floor; it was just that she wasn't altogether sure she could easily get off of it if she needed to. And she very much doubted that Wanda or Jack would be much help pulling her up.

The game wrapped up, as it usually did, with Jack annihilating the block tower with the dump truck.

"You got it, Jack!" said Myrtle.

Jack looked very pleased. But then, just a bit sad that the beautiful block tower had tumbled into ruins.

Wanda croaked in her cigarette-ruined voice, "Wanna play a game, Jack?" She held up a memory game.

Jack did. And so the preschooler and the psychic played Memory. Myrtle had the feeling that this was a game Wanda could win blindfolded. However, somehow, Jack won every time and crowed with joy.

Myrtle said, "Jack, I saved a few very special ornaments for you to put on the tree." She took out a small box that was decades old. "These are ornaments your daddy made when he was about your age."

Jack's eyes widened as he looked in the old box. One ornament was a photograph of his father when he was a little guy. The picture was set in the middle of some glued-together popsicle sticks that had been rather wildly decorated with markers. Reverently, the boy took the ornament and hung it carefully on a very low-hanging branch. Myrtle was glad that Pasha was such a good girl and wouldn't bat at it the next time she came in. Pasha seemed to enjoy *climbing* the tree, but was excellent about not destroying ornaments.

When Elaine arrived to pick up Jack, she found Myrtle and Jack sitting on the sofa together with Myrtle reading an old version of *A Visit from St. Nicholas*. Jack was chuckling over Tasha Tudor's illustrations of a corgi frolicking with Santa.

Elaine moved near them as Myrtle geared up for the grand finale in a very Santa voice, "*Happy Christmas to all, and to all, a good night!*"

Jack gave a happy sigh. "Santa."

"Yes, Santa is making his list and checking it twice," said Elaine. "We should make sure our chimney is all clean for him."

Jack nodded solemnly and reached out his hand to his mother, who took it. She gave Myrtle and Wanda a grateful look. "Thanks, you two."

"We had a blast," said Myrtle. "And Jack somehow managed to beat Wanda at Memory a million times."

"Quite a feat indeed," said Elaine wryly.

"Did you get all your shopping taken care of?" asked Myrtle.

"I think so. I guess I need to take a page out of Santa's book and make a list," said Elaine with a chuckle.

The two left, hand-in-hand.

Myrtle said, "You know, that was really fun. But now I do feel extraordinarily tired."

"Wanna jest eat some supper and then wind down for the day?" asked Wanda.

"You've nailed it. I think a quiet night is in store for us."

And it was. Wanda played solitaire and Myrtle read her book until she couldn't stay awake any longer. It was the first sound night's sleep she'd had in a long while, despite the frenzied prancing of snowflakes on her walls from Erma's light show.

Chapter Nineteen

The next morning, Elaine called Myrtle first thing.

"Elaine? Need help with something?"

Elaine said, "I'm actually calling because I want to help *you* with something. You've been so great to drop everything and lend me a hand lately that I woke up today feeling like I needed to return the favor."

"Well, isn't that sweet! Not that you had to do that, of course. It's always a treat to watch Jack and helping with the Christmas pageant was very interesting." Myrtle fudged just a bit on the pageant.

"Regardless, I'd like to do it. Is there anywhere I can drive you today? That's one thing I do extraordinarily well—drive. I feel like I'm in the car half the day, anyway." Elaine gave a breezy laugh.

"Hmm. I hadn't actually planned my day out, but I was thinking yesterday that I'd like to buy Jack a red wagon for Christmas. All children should have a red wagon. Then he can pull it around the backyard and put acorns and sticks and such in there."

"I think that's really sweet, Myrtle. He'd love it. He's always picking up rocks outside and putting them in a place of honor in his room. So, the hardware store, then? I think I saw wagons for sale there."

Elaine pulled up in the minivan minutes later into Myrtle's driveway. Myrtle climbed in the front seat and turned around to beam at Jack, but Jack wasn't in his seat. "What happened to Jack?"

"Oh, he's playing with a friend of his at the friend's house. A playdate."

Although Myrtle was glad to hear that Jack had friends, she felt a little sad that he was old enough to have them and to go out on playdates.

Elaine drove them over to the hardware shop. The store was well over one hundred years old, with mainly the same family in charge of it. They stocked everything from seeds to baby chicks to tools. You could also pick up an old-fashioned soda like Cheerwine or Blenheim Ginger Ale.

The wagons were right up front, near the sleds. Myrtle said, "I think they're always overly optimistic about the sledding forecast. We haven't had snow here in forever." She paused. "Jack does have a sled, doesn't he?"

Elaine looked as if she might be concerned Myrtle would go over her Christmas budget. "He has Red's old one, yes."

Myrtle looked pleased at that. "That was a good sled, I remember . . . a Flexible Flyer. Although even Red didn't get to use it that often, with the lack of snow. All right, so we'll just get the wagon."

But before they could take it up front to get it checked out, a voice behind them said, "Hello, ladies!"

They turned to see Edgar standing there. "Good to see you both." He held up some towel rods. "I'm just picking up some things for Glynis's house. I've got to change things up a little while I'm there. Make the place my own."

Myrtle thought that was rather ambitious of him, considering the house technically *wasn't* his own.

He gave Elaine a wink. "This must be Red's wife, then?"

Elaine gave him a small smile, and Myrtle pressed her lips together in annoyance at Edgar. "Yes, this is Elaine. The police chief's wife." She said the last bit as something of a reminder.

"A pleasure to meet you," he said with a grin. He looked again at Myrtle. "And you look very nice today, Miss Myrtle."

"Why, thank you. And I'll be getting a new hairdo later, courtesy of your daughter. Faith always does a fine job."

Edgar said, "She's a nice girl, isn't she? Hope Faith will be less stressed than she was when I spoke to her yesterday. She was all tensed up and ready to snap my head off." He chortled at the thought.

"What was Faith upset about yesterday?" asked Elaine.

Edgar gave her another big grin. "Oh, just this investigation. She's ready for it all to be over with. The cops have been asking lots of questions and making her worried she's a suspect. That's the last thing she wants right now when she's trying to start out life with a new husband."

"I'm sure the police are just doing their jobs. Since Nash died, they'd have to go around and speak again to everyone they'd interviewed the first time," said Myrtle.

Edgar nodded. "That's what I told Faith, too. But she wasn't in any mood to speak to me at the time and she got off the phone really fast."

Myrtle could easily imagine how that could be the case. She said, "Of course, she didn't really know Nash, so the police shouldn't be very interested in her."

Edgar lifted his eyebrows in surprise. "Didn't really know him, you said?"

"Isn't that the case?"

Edgar said slowly, "Not true. She was the one who introduced Nash to Glynis."

Myrtle grew still. She and Elaine looked at each other.

"Nash told me that himself, before his untimely death," continued Edgar. "He said Faith had cut his hair a few times. She'd thought he and Glynis had a lot in common."

"Which I guess they did. At least, they seemed to," said Elaine.

Myrtle frowned. "I thought you really didn't know Nash, yourself."

Edgar lifted up his hands as if he were surrendering. "Hey, I didn't say I knew the guy. Just that we'd talked. I saw him in town a couple of days ago and went up to say hi. You know, I'm starting out in a new place and it doesn't hurt to network. Anyway, I'd asked how he and my sister had met and he told me it was Faith." He glanced at his watch. "Guess I better be going. I've got to check this stuff out and install the rods. See you around."

Myrtle watched him thoughtfully as he left. "He's one of those people who always knows what's going on in a town."

Elaine said, "Then he should probably watch his back. If he even *thinks* he knows who's responsible for those two deaths, then he's in a lot of danger."

A leering face suddenly popped up next to them. "Hi there," sang Erma.

Elaine jumped, and Myrtle gasped in dismay. The last thing she wanted today was a visit from Erma. As a matter of fact, her schedule *never* allowed for a visit from Erma.

Edgar hastily prompted the man at the register to speed things up a bit.

Elaine and Myrtle were well and truly trapped, however.

"Saw you talking to Edgar," said Erma in a loud voice that she fondly considered a whisper.

Edgar turned around, frowning. Clearly, he wanted to be the one to dispense gossip. He did not enjoy being the target of it.

Erma pantomimed drinking, giving them both a wink. "I saw him drinking from a flask outside the store before he came in."

Elaine looked as if she wasn't sure how to react, and Myrtle shrugged. "None of my business."

Erma apparently didn't like her gossiping to be discounted. She said, "He does it all the time. He was even drinking from a flask at his daughter's wedding reception."

"As I said, it's none of my business." Myrtle was becoming cross. It was amazing how quickly her mood could change from one second to another.

But Erma was determined to dispense her knowledge. "But there's one thing I do know. At the wedding? He wasn't as drunk as he seemed. He's far drunker right now."

Edgar was still at the cash register, and Myrtle could see that his neck was flushed.

She said quietly, "That seems ambitious of him since he appeared to be passed out at the reception."

"He wasn't!" protested Erma. "He looked like he was, but it was all for show. I could see the light from his phone when he was slumped over. He was on his phone!"

Edgar, now finished at the checkout counter, quickly slipped out the door. Myrtle only wished she could do the same.

Myrtle still didn't seem impressed by this. This spurred Erma to take drastic measures. "Say, have I told you about my last trip to the doctor, Myrtle? You won't believe what he found wrong with me."

Myrtle raised her hand. "I can't be dealing with this nonsense today, Erma. Elaine has been kind enough to drive me on my errands and now she needs to drop me home so she can pick up Jack from his playdate."

Erma looked crestfallen as Myrtle and Elaine hurried away to the cash register with the red wagon. Elaine helped her load it into the minivan, and then they drove off.

Chapter Twenty

"**D**o you want to keep the wagon at your place or mine?" asked Elaine.

"Oh, I think I should probably keep it at mine, don't you think? It's not as if a wagon can really be concealed very well. Jack might come across it at your house and want to take it on a pre-Christmas spin."

Elaine said, "That makes sense. But for now, how about if we keep it in the car? I'd like to take you to run another errand."

"Wouldn't you rather do your own shopping? It's so close to Christmas."

"You were a tremendous help with the play, Myrtle. I'd like to pay you back, if I can."

Elaine sounded determined, so Myrtle considered the question of where to go. It would be good to have another conversation with Faith and she *was* in need of a visit to the salon. "I've been thinking I need to get my wash and set."

Elaine said, "You want to get your hair done? Do you have an appointment with Faith?'

"I don't, actually, because I keep forgetting to make one with everything going on. But there's a sign on the door of the Beauty

Box that says they take walk-ins. I've always wanted to test that theory."

Elaine paused. "You don't think getting a walk-in slot this close to Christmas would be a problem?"

"It shouldn't be. If they can't accommodate walk-ins, they should take the sign down, shouldn't they?"

Elaine didn't appear to want to argue the point. "I'm happy to take you there and pick you up. Would you like to go now, or have me pick you up later?"

"There's no time like the present. Besides, it's nice and early. They should have plenty of availability now."

However, when Myrtle walked into the Beauty Box, it appeared to be quite crowded with ladies. Even more disconcerting, Faith seemed to be dyeing some woman's hair; a process Myrtle knew could take ages. Cat, the owner, waved to her as she washed someone's hair at the sink.

Faith looked startled when she spotted Myrtle coming in through the door. "Miss Myrtle! Did I mess up? Do we have an appointment right now?"

Myrtle shook her head. "I've forgotten to make one for my wash and set and I'm not sure I can make it through Christmas with my hair this wild. I look like Einstein. Can you fit me in?"

Faith said, "I can squeeze you in while my color appointment is processing. Would you like to take a seat?"

Myrtle did. Unfortunately, she hadn't brought a book with her, so had to make do with a pile of rather ratty-looking magazines. She flipped through them, only stopping when she saw a recipe that seemed tempting. And it claimed it was easy, too.

Myrtle surreptitiously tore the recipe out of the magazine and stuffed it into her huge purse.

The Beauty Box had gone all-out in terms of Christmas decorations. It was difficult to determine whether Bo's Diner or the salon had the most, or tackiest, decorations. Someone seemed to have an addiction to snowmen. Myrtle thought it probably wasn't Cat, the owner of the salon . . . it was a bit cutesy for her. There were snowmen and snowwomen of every conceivable variety decorating every nook and cranny of the shop. Myrtle had the feeling that they were chosen because they could conceivably stay up long after Christmas was over.

She was contemplating the longevity of snowmen decorations when Faith came up breathlessly to her. "Ready?"

"Hmm?" asked Myrtle. "Oh, right. Yes, the wash-and-set."

Faith was a wonderful hairdresser, decided Myrtle. She always enjoyed getting her hair washed by her and the scalp massages she gave. And Faith was always thoughtful enough to put a folded towel behind Myrtle's neck at the sink, so she had a cushion there.

Once Myrtle was in the chair, she said, "How have you been doing, Faith? I've been thinking about you. Especially since Nash perished. I've been meaning to come by with a casserole or some such."

Faith swiftly said, "No need for that, Miss Myrtle. The church's care committee brought by so much food that Holden and I won't have to cook for months. I appreciate it, though. I've been doing all right, but I have to say that it's all been pretty stressful."

"Of course it has. I can only imagine trying to start out with a new chapter under these circumstances. And the probate process is quite daunting."

Myrtle assessed Faith's image in the mirror. She certainly did look tired and drained. "It's not just probate, though, is it? It's also the investigation. I'm sure it's been exhausting."

Faith's eyes met hers in the mirror. "To be honest, it really has been. Miss Myrtle, I hate to ask you this, but do you have any idea what Red might be thinking right now? He doesn't believe Holden and I are suspects, does he?"

Myrtle sighed. "Sadly, Faith, I never know what's going through Red's mind. It was that way even when he was a little guy. He's been asking you questions about Nash's death I'm guessing?"

Faith gently combed Myrtle's hair. "That's right. Of course, I knew he should. Nash was involved with Glynis, and it looks like the two . . . deaths are related." Faith stumbled over the word *deaths* a bit.

Myrtle looked at Faith's drawn features in the mirror. "It's been hard, hasn't it?"

To Myrtle's alarm, Faith teared up. But before Myrtle could get her arms out from the cape and grab her purse for a tissue, Faith reached across to a handy tissue box right across from her.

After scrubbing at her eyes, Faith gave Myrtle a rueful look. "Sorry."

"You don't have a single thing to be sorry about," said Myrtle stoutly.

Faith took a deep breath. "Thanks. You're always so sensible, Miss Myrtle. I think that it's only just hit me in the last day or so that Glynis is gone. She's always been so strong and hardy and . . . there. The funeral finally drove the point home that she's not coming back. I'm not going to say that Glynis and I had the perfect relationship, or anything. She could be really hard on me. But she did always want what was best for me. And she raised me when my own dad couldn't be bothered."

"She was family, dear, wasn't she? And no matter how much family might drive us crazy, they're still *family*." Myrtle paused. "'Thinking back to Nash. Were you able to give Red and Lieutenant Perkins a good alibi? That would have definitely helped get them off your back, at least for the time being."

Faith looked uncertain. "I'm not sure how strong they thought my alibi was. It was basically Holden vouching for me, and vice versa. We were at home with each other when Nash died. Holden had cooked a special meal, which was great. He's actually an excellent cook. I know we have tons of food from the church, but Holden thought if he cooked something that it might calm his nerves a little bit."

"He's been on edge, too?"

Faith nodded. "We both have. It's just a lot of stress, you know. I mean, planning the funeral wasn't at all stressful, because Glynis had outlined everything to the T. But I still needed to meet with the minister, make sure the reception was planned out, and stuff like that. I've also started the probate process, and have been dealing with my dad." She rolled her eyes.

"Edgar's been a pain, has he?" asked Myrtle.

"Naturally. Sorry if I sound sarcastic. It's just that I remember being a little girl and he'd say he was going to join Glynis and me for Christmas. I'd be *so* excited, you know? Instead of spending Christmas morning in my pjs like other kids, I'd get all dressed up, ready for my dad. We'd wait for him before I opened my stocking or any presents. I could always see Glynis getting more and more annoyed as the morning wore on. She'd suggest that I unwrap everything, but I'd tell her I was sure he was coming soon. And he wouldn't." Faith shrugged. "And now? He's showed up right before Christmas and seems to have absolutely no plans on leaving."

"And this time, you're ready for him to leave?"

Faith gave a low chuckle. "You guessed it. Life is funny, isn't it?"

"No wonder you and Holden are on edge. Hopefully, cooking dinner helped him out."

Faith said, "It did. Then, just because we've been so exhausted, we turned in for an early night. I'm not sure Red totally believed us, but that's what happened. Like I said, it's probably not much of an alibi for Nash's murder."

"What did you think of Nash's relationship with Glynis?"

"Well, in some ways, they were really well-suited. They both enjoyed the same kinds of books, movies, and music. But you know sometimes how relationships are sort of lopsided?"

Myrtle asked, "You mean, when one person cares more deeply than the other?"

"That's right. I got the feeling that Nash cared a lot more about Glynis than she did for him. I don't think she thought of Nash as a *fling*, but I don't think she was all that serious about him."

"It sounds like you're right, considering the fact that she ended the relationship," said Myrtle.

"Exactly. And Nash didn't want to give it up. He was driving her crazy, trying to get her to come back to him. He should have known that the way he was pestering her was going to push her away from him, instead."

Myrtle asked, "Did you know Nash fairly well?"

"I never even saw him when he wasn't with Glynis. I wouldn't say I really knew him." Faith carefully rolled curlers into Myrtle's hair after applying a styling cream. "I just know Glynis was furious when he turned up at the reception."

"Yes, well, that wasn't appropriate, no matter the situation. Gatecrashing a wedding? That's in very poor taste." Myrtle sniffed. She had no problems at all gatecrashing a cookie swap, but weddings were entirely different. She paused. "I was speaking with someone who mentioned something about Glynis having an outsized ego. I wouldn't have thought that myself, but was that something you'd noticed?"

Faith said dryly, "I can tell you must have been talking with my father. Sure, I think Glynis had a healthy ego. But didn't she deserve to? She and Edgar were raised by the same people, in the same house, and look how they turned out. My dad has never stuck with a job in his life. And Glynis was completely the opposite. She had all this drive to go to school and have a successful career."

"She could be a bit outspoken, couldn't she?" asked Myrtle.

Faith finished with the curlers and surveyed her handiwork. "Glynis could. She had a habit of speaking her mind, which created problems sometimes."

"The way she spoke at the reception, for instance?"

"Right. Glynis was bound and determined to share what she thought the truth about Holden was. But she was self-centered enough not to realize that wasn't the right setting for it." Faith made a face, remembering.

Myrtle asked, "Did Red ask you if you had any ideas about who might have murdered Nash?"

Faith shook her head. "He didn't. But I can't help thinking Belinda Clark might have had something to do with it. I really like Belinda; I do her hair, actually. But I feel like she lost her mind over Nash."

"When he ended their relationship, you mean?"

"That's right. I couldn't believe how angry Belinda got. She was practically seething while I was doing her hair," said Faith.

Myrtle said, "Belinda seemed to think she and Nash were in a very serious relationship."

Faith led Myrtle over to a dryer chair and sat her down. "That's the thing, though. Even I could tell Nash probably wasn't that serious. I'd see them out at lunch together and Nash would be on his phone and Belinda would be talking to him with this sort of starstruck expression on her face. But he never seemed like he was actually paying that much attention to her. I started wondering if this dream relationship she thought she was in was all in her head."

"Bless her heart," said Myrtle.

Faith nodded. "When she'd come in here, she'd have these wedding magazines. She'd flip through the pages, picking out her favorite hair styles. Belinda would talk about the type of dress she was planning on buying and we'd mull over what hair style would work best with it. I mean, we had a total strategy set up for the wedding. It was a while before I figured out that the two of them weren't even engaged."

"Mercy."

Faith sighed. "I had absolutely no idea Nash was going to dump Belinda to go out with my aunt."

"Well, of course you didn't! Did Belinda think you had?"

"I guess she thought I knew something about Glynis and Nash prior to it happening. Maybe she thought I'd seen Nash at Glynis's house or something. Anyway, she seemed to think I was aware of it and was making fun of her behind her back for being naïve. She changed stylists once Nash left her."

Myrtle's eyes widened. "Really? A change of stylist in Bradley is very much like a divorce. It's a really radical move."

"I was very hurt by it," said Faith, shaking her head. "I hadn't been anything but supportive of Belinda. I mean, I was right there with her when she was coming up with her dream wedding."

Myrtle asked, "Did she talk with you about your own wedding?"

"Sure. We'd talk about the different vendors I was using—who was helping with the flowers or the food or stuff like that." Faith shrugged. "I have the feeling Belinda was setting herself up for a fall, you know. All those plans. All the *details* of all the plans. She'd built it all up so much and then, when Nash started seeing Glynis, it was like she'd lost a dream instead of just a relationship."

Myrtle said, "Do you think Nash was that much of a catch?"

Faith snorted. "No. I mean, everyone has their problems to work through, of course. But it's silly that Belinda was so determined that Nash was The One. Anybody could tell he had a tough job staying faithful. Everybody has their problems, of course. But everybody wasn't as flawed as Nash."

"Holden has his problems, too?" asked Myrtle in a sweetly innocent voice. She thought of the gambling that Georgia had said Holden had done.

"He used to, yes. But those are in the past and I'm so proud of him for overcoming them." Faith paused, messing with the controls of the dryer before turning it on. "Okay, Miss Myrtle. Let's get your hair dry before you catch a cold."

Myrtle was again sorry that she hadn't brought her book with her. She picked up another tattered magazine. It professed many opinions about the way celebrities dressed when they went out to various events or even to the grocery store. Since Myrtle didn't know who the celebrities were and cared very little for fashion, she soon found herself nodding off under the dryer.

Before she knew it, Faith was shepherding her back into the chair to take the curlers out and brush and lightly spray her hair. Myrtle texted Elaine, who came right by to pick her up.

"Your hair looks beautiful!" said Elaine, peering at Faith's creation next to her in the minivan.

"It does. Sadly, my hair doesn't seem to want to behave itself unless Faith is in charge of it. It gets all sassy when it's just me. I'm sure at some point in the night tonight, it will revert to its old ways. It's generally incorrigible."

Elaine took Myrtle back to her house, and they got the wagon squirreled away into a closet. Wanda had apparently gone for a walk; she'd left a scrawled, rather cryptic note in her best phonetic approximation of writing. After Elaine left, Myrtle settled down at her computer. She wasn't pleased by the fact that a relative newcomer to town like Edgar appeared to know so much about people in Bradley. Perhaps she could correct that by googling the various suspects.

Fifteen minutes later, she decided the people of Bradley either cared little about their search-engine-optimization or else were boring enough not to have much of an online profile. Myrtle herself had quite a few entries to her name. After all, she was a star reporter for the *Bradley Bugle*. Glynis had a smattering of links relating to her work. Nash's online profile comprised various certifications and information on the hospital website.

When she got to Belinda, though, Myrtle made some surprising discoveries. Like the others, Belinda was mostly identifiable on the internet through her work—her tax service and work as a CPA. But on the listing for her office, there was an absolutely terrible review—a scathing one—written by a G. Ross. It had to be Glynis, decided Myrtle. It not only intimated that Belinda was an incompetent CPA, but it also stated that Belinda was slow to return phone calls and didn't check her messages often.

Myrtle considered this. The fact of the matter was that Glynis had a lot of clout in Bradley while she was living. She had a good deal of money, was smart, and wasn't afraid to speak her mind. In a place like Bradley, that equated to power. But not just power—influence, too. Belinda would have been most distressed to discover a review like that one from someone like Glynis. Upset enough to eliminate Glynis altogether? It seemed possible.

At this point, Wanda returned from her walk. She had a happy glow about her. "Got to see Jack again. Cute kid."

"Isn't he? He's the best. I think he's going to love his red wagon, too. Can't you just see him putting a collection of rocks in there?"

They had a quiet, peaceful evening together. Wanda cooked again, this time a pasta dish, which they consumed in front of the TV. They caught up on *Tomorrow's Promise* and marveled at the way the show's writers had turned a regular Christmas party into the opportunity for Samantha, the amnesiac, to wander in after being missing for weeks and create complete havoc.

After a while, they turned in. Wanda seemed to be an excellent sleeper and Myrtle, although very envious, was trying to do better herself despite the craziness of Erma's glaring lights on her walls. She drifted off after reading in bed for a few minutes . . . a testament to the busyness of the week.

She woke up sometime later to the sound of alarmed squeaking. Myrtle frowned groggily, trying to remember why the squeaking could possibly be important. Then she sat up in bed. The little mouse. It must have been caught in the trap and was causing a fuss because of it.

Sure enough, as soon as she walked into the living room, she saw the small creature in the trap, completely unharmed but quite anxious. Myrtle decided Erma's yard would make for a wonderful place for the mouse to run free. Perhaps the mouse would even decide to check in and see what kinds of snacks Erma had available in her kitchen. Due to Erma's assorted medical issues, Myrtle had the feeling that there were all sorts of unhealthy items in there.

Myrtle gently picked up the trap and walked outside the front door with it. The moon and stars were out, but were completely overwhelmed by Erma's garish display. Myrtle tightened her lips and squared her shoulders. She remembered Wanda's words to her: *if you want something done, do it yourself.*

She opened the trap, and the little creature scampered away with great relief. Then Myrtle quietly walked toward the nexus of the cords in Erma's yard, intending on giving herself at least one night of peaceful sleep.

Then she stopped, peering into the darkness. There was a sound, a rustling. Way too big to be the mouse she'd just freed. Was another neighbor just as fed up as she'd been with the lights?

As she drew closer, however, she saw the dark figure didn't seem intent on pulling out the cords and ending the light show. Instead, it appeared to be working on opening a window.

"You!" yelled Myrtle.

The figure spun around, and the circulating lights momentarily caught the startled features of Edgar Ross.

Chapter Twenty-One

"What are you doing here?" he grated in a gasping voice. "A good deed," said Myrtle with a sniff. "What are *you* doing here? Something nefarious, I gather."

"Be quiet," Edgar growled. "I'm warning you."

Myrtle, unlike most of her peers, had never smoked. She was quite proud of her lung capacity and demonstrated it by hollering, "Why? Because you're worried RED might hear us? Don't you know he lives right across the street from me?"

With great satisfaction, Myrtle saw lights instantly go on across the street. Red, similar to his mother, was a rather light sleeper.

Edgar lunged at Myrtle, a furious expression on his face. But Myrtle neatly sidestepped him, aided by her cane. Edgar, on the other hand, became twisted in the knotty mess of Erma's many electrical cords and tumbled ignominiously to the ground with a thump.

Floodlights turned on from the side of the house and Erma, crowned by curlers, came flying out, her mouth gaping as she took in the sight of Edgar tangled in her Christmas cords, Myrtle looking scornfully down at him, and Pasha, who'd silently arrived in the darkness and was scowling at Edgar.

Edgar tried to scramble up, but became even more embroiled in the wires. He must have realized the game was over when Red, looking very grouchy indeed, suddenly showed up in a pair of Christmas pajamas that looked like something Elaine had made during a past, disastrous hobby.

"What's going on here?" demanded Red. His eyes narrowed as he recognized Edgar lying on the ground. "You know, Edgar, I can't think of a single good reason why you'd be here in Erma's yard."

Erma, who'd backed away to a safe, Pasha-free place, said, "I don't know *what* he's doing here, Red."

"I know," said Myrtle smugly. "And, in the meantime, I suggest you put Edgar in a safe place for questioning so I can tell you all about it."

Edgar had a hangdog expression about him as Red arrested him for trespassing. "Until other charges are added," growled Red, still cantankerous about being awakened. He called the state police as his deputy pulled up and took Edgar away.

Miles staggered out of his house during the ruckus and joined Myrtle, Wanda, Pasha, and Red in Erma's yard. Erma, leery of Pasha, had hung back to give her own statement to the state police when they showed up.

Myrtle had just settled down on her sofa when Lieutenant Perkins walked in the door. Compared to Red, he looked amazingly professional, as if he'd known he was going to be awakened at three in the morning. At least Red had managed to change from Christmas pajamas to his uniform. It was just unfortunate that his red hair was standing on end.

"Mrs. Clover," Lieutenant Perkins said, "I understand you cracked another case for us."

"And just about got her head cracked open in the process," grumbled Red.

Myrtle ignored her son. "I certainly did, Lieutenant Perkins."

Red wasn't ready to stop giving her a hard time. "So you spotted Edgar Ross lurking around Erma's house and decided to take him down all on your own? Even with the police chief right next door?"

"Absolutely not," said Myrtle, glowering at him. "I'm decidedly *not* stupid, thank you very much. I was heading over to turn off Erma's light display."

"Of course you were," said Red, rubbing his eyes.

Wanda intoned, "Want somethin' done, you gotta do it yourself."

Red squinted at Wanda.

"Anyway, as soon as I spotted Edgar there, I knew precisely why he was outside Erma's house. He overheard Erma and me talking in the hardware store."

Now Red looked very confused. "Wait. You were having a conversation with Erma?"

"It wasn't voluntary. Anyway, you know how loud she is. She was bellowing at me that Edgar wasn't drunk at the wedding reception at all. Erma intimated he was faking it—that when he was slumped over a table, he was actually on his phone. She'd seen the light from his phone."

Perkins looked thoughtful. "Couldn't that have just been Edgar's idea of a relaxing pose to catch up with social media?"

"It could have been. But I also wondered if he was playing up being drunk at the wedding. I think he used it as an alibi . . . if everyone at the wedding testified that Edgar was falling-down drunk, it meant that he couldn't possibly have been able to track down Glynis, hit her with a champagne bottle, and then return to the party as if nothing had happened."

Perkins nodded. "And money was the motive?"

"Absolutely. You should have seen how excited he was to re-decorate Glynis's house and make it his own. I don't think he really thought about Glynis one way or another. It wasn't as if Edgar's feelings were hurt by the way she treated him, like Holden's were. Glynis's death was simply the means to an end. Edgar was clearly not fond of working. He's getting older and the idea of settling down and living a life of ease probably appealed to him."

Perkins said, "Nash must have been onto him."

Myrtle shrugged. "He was a doctor. I'd imagine it would be very hard to *stop* being a physician, even when you were gate-crashing a reception. Nash might have realized Edgar was simply playing a part, in terms of being drunk."

"Didn't he realize it pretty late?" asked Red dubiously. "He could have told us when we questioned him that Faith's father wasn't as messed up as he'd appeared."

"I believe he was more preoccupied by Glynis's tragic death and the fact that he was suddenly seen as a suspect," said Myrtle. "Then, later, he might have realized it would benefit him if he could cast aspersions on someone else. Unfortunately, he must have accidentally indicated he knew something about Edgar's involvement. Edgar might not have been as smart as Nash, but he was wily. He'd have noticed if Nash were acting differently around him."

Perkins nodded. "And tonight? How did you get embroiled in all this?"

Pasha brushed against Myrtle's leg as if realizing the night could have turned out very differently.

Miles nodded, leaning forward to find out how Myrtle had so surprisingly ended up in Erma's yard.

"Well, it all started with Erma's obnoxious Christmas lights," said Myrtle darkly. "Red, I'm surprised you didn't shut those things down long ago."

Red sighed. "Complaining about lights didn't seem to fit the Christmas spirit, Mama."

"You know my bedroom is right on the side of the house. Those blasted snowflakes have been psychedelically dancing on my walls for days. I've been getting more and more agitated each day."

"I can confirm that," said Miles.

"Plus, I had a mouse in the house. Just a little creature."

Red frowned. "A mouse? You never told me that. Usually if there's one mouse, there are plenty more."

"Not in this particular instance. Pasha brought it in, the dear."

Perkins asked, "Pasha?"

"My feral cat. Well, she's not really *mine*. Pasha belongs to herself. She's right there."

They all turned to look at Pasha, who'd been eyeing the group with interest. Now, seeing everyone's eyes on her, she quickly climbed Myrtle's Christmas tree and peered out at them from the branches.

"She's a bit shy. But she's been cleverly engaged in her very own version of *The Twelve Days of Christmas*."

Red rubbed his temples as if they'd started pounding.

"Pasha brings me a gift every day. The gifts can be rather startling, as the live mouse was. But Holden kindly provided me with a humane trap with which I could catch the errant mouse."

Red said darkly, "Holden did? That sounds more like you being nosy, Mama."

Myrtle straightened in her chair. "As if! I can't help it if he works for the only exterminator in town."

"Can we get back to how you ended up at Erma's? All I'm hearing about are snowflake lights and mice," asked Red in a pleading voice.

"I was just getting to that point. As I was saying, Holden gave me a wonderful trap. I heard some alarmed squeaking a little while ago and realized the mouse had been caught and needed to be set free outside. Naturally, I chose Erma's yard to set the little guy free in."

"Naturally," said Miles with a smile.

"You'll be glad to know the mouse was just fine. Anyway, while I was over there, I had this sudden urge to unplug Erma's light show. I needed to have one night of decent sleep. It *is* Christmas, after all."

"So you decided to trespass," said Red, rolling his eyes.

"I decided to take care of myself and my sleep requirements. But as I stepped over toward the side of her house, I spotted Edgar there, intent on breaking in."

Perkins slowly said, "He was there to keep Erma from disclosing to anyone else that he hadn't really been intoxicated at the wedding reception. But then, he'd have had to come after you, too."

Myrtle shrugged. "I live right next door. It would have been convenient for him. He lunged for me, but got caught up in the mess of wires and cords that Erma had strewn around. Hoisted by his own petard."

Wanda sighed. "Greedy."

"*Very* greedy," said Myrtle. "And now he'll be spending time in jail. It's just as well for the young couple. They didn't need to be starting out their life together with Edgar lurking around all the time, asking for money and generally being a nuisance."

"Or killing people," added Miles.

"That too." Myrtle turned to look at Perkins. "Now that this case is all wrapped up, I hope you'll be able to head back home and have a wonderful Christmas with your family. It's a pity this investigation was so close to the holiday."

He gave her a warm smile. "With your help, I'll definitely be home for Christmas."

Minutes later, Red and Perkins left to question Edgar at the station.

Myrtle looked at the clock. "I just realized it's now Christmas Eve. Are we going to go back to sleep or are we up for the day?"

Wanda grated, "Think I'm up."

Miles nodded. "But a cup of coffee wouldn't go amiss. I'll make it."

"You won't . . . I'm the hostess. Besides, I'm the whole reason you're both awake right now."

Myrtle bustled into the kitchen to make a pot of coffee. When she returned, she had a small gift with her. She saw Wanda had a couple of small presents on her lap.

"You knew I was going to pull gifts out?" asked Myrtle with a smile. "But don't you want to wait until tomorrow? I can put mine for you under the tree."

Pasha peered out of the tree branches thoughtfully.

Wanda shook her head. "Let's do 'em now. Kinda fun to do them a day early."

Miles said, "Unfortunately, I'm *not* a psychic and didn't realize we were doing this now."

Myrtle smiled at him. "You mean at four o'clock in the morning on Christmas Eve? How shortsighted of you, Miles! Nevertheless, I think your present is one you should open now. You might be able to make some use of it. I'll wait for mine for Christmas."

Miles said, "I do actually have my gift for Wanda with me. I pulled on my slacks from yesterday and it was in there."

Myrtle very much suspected that his gift for Wanda might be cash.

He did indeed have an envelope for Wanda. It was slightly crumpled from its time in Miles's pocket. He'd carefully written her name on it, though, and tried to make it festive by drawing a Christmas tree on it. The Christmas tree had an odd resemblance to a cactus somehow.

Wanda took it gratefully, though. Then she handed hers to Miles. He smiled at her and opened it. When he'd dropped her off at the dollar store, she'd gotten him a gift, too. He saw it was a jolly looking bottle of hand sanitizer, covered with Santas and trees.

Miles looked pleased. "Thank you, Wanda." He took a delicate sniff. "The fragrance is very nice, too. Not too heavy on alcohol."

"I do believe you're a connoisseur of hand sanitizers," said Myrtle.

Miles nodded. Then he looked concerned. "Wait. Does this mean I need to use them, Wanda? Am I going to come in contact with some germs?"

He frowned, looking around him as if visible germs were going to leap out at him and attack him from behind Myrtle's furniture.

Wanda hastily said, "Jest a gift. No illness in sight."

Miles breathed a sigh of relief.

"Now you open yers," said Wanda, bobbing her head gently at Myrtle.

Myrtle loved opening presents and opened hers with enthusiasm. It had been carefully wrapped in a foil gift wrap that reflected the Christmas tree bulbs on it. When she opened it, she saw two gifts there: a large magnifying glass that would have made Sherlock Holmes envious and a new measuring cup.

"Aren't you clever? I haven't been able to measure ingredients exactly for a little while after Puddin smashed my measuring cup when she was 'cleaning up,'" said Myrtle. "And I'll keep the magnifying glass on my coffee table. Not only will it help me out with any pesky small print, it will also remind Red who the real detective is. Now you open my present, Wanda."

Wanda did. When she unwrapped it, a small chess game was revealed.

Myrtle beamed at it. "Isn't it the cutest? Now you don't have to wait until Miles finally makes a move in your remote chess game. You can play this little computer by yourself. And you don't even have to buy batteries for it—it's rechargeable." Myrtle looked very pleased with herself.

Wanda peered at it and then grinned her big, gap-toothed grin. "Thank you."

Then Myrtle pointed out a rather large present from under the Christmas tree. "That one's for you, Miles. Merry Christmas."

Miles blinked at it. "I thought you just said we'd wait to exchange our gifts for each other."

"I said I didn't need my present now. Nevertheless, I think *your* present is one you should open now. You might make some use of it."

Miles walked up to the tree as Pasha gave him a suspicious look through the branches. He paused, looking at her a bit leerily as Wanda and Myrtle grinned at each other.

Myrtle said, "She won't bother you at all. Pasha just thinks you might be coming to get her out of the tree. And that's making her sad."

Miles looked directly at Pasha and said in a fervent voice, "I don't want to get you out of the tree."

Pasha still seemed doubtful of his intentions and narrowed her eyes in a warning way.

Miles took the present and settled back in a chair. He unwrapped it by carefully removing the pieces of tape and unfolding the sides and the middle.

Myrtle rolled her eyes at Wanda at Miles's deliberate process but didn't say a word.

When Miles finally unwrapped the gift, he stared at it. "A tabletop Christmas tree," he said slowly.

Myrtle looked very pleased with herself. "It's a way of enjoying a tree without having the *trouble* of a tree. I didn't much care for the thought of you sitting at home without a Christmas tree. It all seemed sort of . . . barren."

Wanda croaked, "Trees is nice. Nice to look at."

Myrtle nodded at her. "That's the thing. When I sit and look at my Christmas tree, it's as if all the Christmases through all the years come back into my mind. It just makes me happy."

Miles gave Myrtle a smile and started to speak. But it seemed he had a hard time making his voice work for the first time. He cleared his throat and said, "Thank you, Myrtle."

Wanda's eyes grew misty.

Myrtle, very much concerned her two friends might suddenly tear up, briskly said, "Now, let's have some breakfast. And perhaps some of that apple cider I picked up at the store . . . I can heat it up on the stove."

"Or the microwave," Miles quickly said, fearing the combination of Myrtle and the stove.

Wanda grinned at him.

And so, when the sun sleepily rose on Christmas Eve and its rays came through the windows, Myrtle and her friends were listening to Christmas music, drinking hot cider, and reminiscing on Christmases past.

About the Author

Elizabeth writes the Southern Quilting mysteries and Memphis Barbeque mysteries for Penguin Random House and the Myrtle Clover series for Midnight Ink and independently. She blogs at ElizabethSpannCraig.com/blog, named by Writer's Digest as one of the 101 Best Websites for Writers. Elizabeth makes her home in Matthews, North Carolina, with her husband. She's the mother of two.

Sign up for Elizabeth's free newsletter to stay updated on releases:

https://bit.ly/2xZUXqO

This and That

I love hearing from my readers. You can find me on Facebook as Elizabeth Spann Craig Author, on Twitter as elizabethscraig, on my website at elizabethspanncraig.com, and by email at elizabethspanncraig@gmail.com.

Thanks so much for reading my book...I appreciate it. If you enjoyed the story, would you please leave a short review on the site where you purchased it? Just a few words would be great. Not only do I feel encouraged reading them, but they also help other readers discover my books. Thank you!

Did you know my books are available in print and ebook formats? Most of the Myrtle Clover series is available in audio and some of the Southern Quilting mysteries are. Find the audiobooks here: https://elizabethspanncraig.com/audio/

Please follow me on BookBub for my reading recommendations and release notifications.

I'd also like to thank some folks who helped me put this book together. Thanks to my cover designer, Karri Klawiter, for her awesome covers. Thanks to my editor, Judy Beatty for her help. Thanks to beta readers Amanda Arrieta, Rebecca Wahr, Cassie Kelley, and Dan Harris for all of their helpful suggestions and careful reading. Thanks to my ARC readers for helping to spread the word. Thanks, as always, to my family and readers.

Other Works by Elizabeth

Myrtle Clover Series in Order (be sure to look for the Myrtle series in audio, ebook, and print):

Pretty is as Pretty Dies

Progressive Dinner Deadly

A Dyeing Shame

A Body in the Backyard

Death at a Drop-In

A Body at Book Club

Death Pays a Visit

A Body at Bunco

Murder on Opening Night

Cruising for Murder

Cooking is Murder

A Body in the Trunk

Cleaning is Murder

Edit to Death

Hushed Up

A Body in the Attic

Murder on the Ballot

Death of a Suitor

A Dash of Murder
Death at a Diner
A Myrtle Clover Christmas
Southern Quilting Mysteries in Order:
Quilt or Innocence
Knot What it Seams
Quilt Trip
Shear Trouble
Tying the Knot
Patch of Trouble
Fall to Pieces
Rest in Pieces
On Pins and Needles
Fit to be Tied
Embroidering the Truth
Knot a Clue
Quilt-Ridden
Needled to Death
A Notion to Murder
Crosspatch
The Village Library Mysteries in Order (Debuting 2019):
Checked Out
Overdue
Borrowed Time
Hush-Hush
Where There's a Will
Frictional Characters
Spine Tingling

A Novel Idea

Memphis Barbeque Mysteries in Order (Written as Riley Adams):

Delicious and Suspicious

Finger Lickin' Dead

Hickory Smoked Homicide

Rubbed Out

And a standalone "cozy zombie" novel: Race to Refuge, written as Liz Craig

Lightning Source UK Ltd.
Milton Keynes UK
UKHW022221191022
410771UK00011B/72